THE
RESCUE OF
DEMISTRATH

THE
RESCUE OF
DEMISTRATH

Rose Stauffer

Library of Congress Control Number:		2020905152
ISBN:	Hardcover	978-1-7960-9435-0
	Softcover	978-1-7960-9434-3
	eBook	978-1-7960-9433-6

Print information available on the last page.

Rev. date: 04/07/2020

To order additional copies of this book, contact:
Xlibris
1-888-795-4274
www.Xlibris.com
Orders@Xlibris.com
808318

To Arlene, my mother
and to the Goddess Gals
of Virginia

You always had the power, my dear.
You just had to learn it
for yourself.

—Glinda, *The Wizard of Oz*

CHAPTER 1

THE PUNGENT PORT-WINE red stain on the rug was shocking, blasted on the old tan Persian carpet like buckshot—bam!—spreading its Rorschach inkblot shape over the gentle creamy canvas of the rug's intricate weavings. Bernadette, my mistress, remained still as the Blue Ridge Mountains, lying on her side in repose on the bed, faced toward the window. Her little bony body only consumed a fraction of the massive four-poster bed, and I couldn't help thinking how all my brothers and sisters and I could sleep in a cozy heap on that bed.

"This is my deathbed, Eva, and so I must finish my time here." She had been faithfully abiding by her pronouncement for days. And here I thought "deathbeds" were more like the last twenty-four hours of a person's life, but never mind. Ms. Bernadette's eccentricity was hers and hers alone, and I knew it well. I'd been her handmaid, her foot soldier, her "step and fetch it" errand girl for the past five years.

This morning, as in all the past seventeen mornings, it was the chamber pot duties that brought me face-to-face with the mess on the carpet. Ms. Bernadette, for the record, was not incontinent, but she preferred to use the bedside commode during the nights. I looked again at the carpet stain. I swear to God if I didn't know any better, I'd say a murder took place on that carpet except minus all the other components: the body, the weapon, the motive. Well, motive probably existed aplenty, but I knew my imagination was having a little fun with me.

I crouched down to examine the stain. Was it wine? Ms. B. wasn't a drinker, but who's to say she wouldn't add it to her deathbed activities? I looked around for a glass, a bottle, a stopper. Shamus in the kitchen was always fixing trays to take to the master of Ferncliff. I'd see Shamus most evenings taking trays loaded with interesting bottles, glasses, and metal instruments to his room.

Finding nothing to affirm my search, I set about the business of drawing back the heavy brocade drapes. Ms. Bernadette stirred ever so slightly, and a weak alto moan signaled she was still of this earth. I turned from the expansive arched window to approach the palatial bed.

"It's morning again, Ms. Bernadette. You've lived to see another day."

Her crepey eyelids fluttered before opening, and I could see the glassy blue of her eyes search around before landing on my face. I reached out to arrange the comforter and waited for the daily marching orders.

Instead, she said, "Tell me, what is your favorite breakfast?"

Ms. Bernadette Robinson and I had a special relationship. Normally, the house staff tried to refrain from personal conversation so as not to draw attention to ourselves and thereby keeping secure the hierarchy of respect for the "master and missus." Even though I was instructed thusly, Ms. B. tended to talk with me in a personal manner when others weren't around. I learned quickly to respond promptly and to the point. At her age, Ms. B. told me, whenever I hesitated, "Time is of the essence, girl. Answer me with something!"

"Poached eggs and buttered toast, ma'am," I said without hesitation.

She eyed me suspiciously as she squirmed to raise herself against her pillows. I quickly stopped my course to the bedside commode and moved back to the bed to assist her.

"How long have I been in my bed?"

"Over two weeks, ma'am."

"A fortnight," I heard her mutter to herself.

She was looking around the room, from her perch in the massive mahogany slab of a bed, the fabric of her white cotton nightgown with billowy sleeves and drawstring collar swirled together with the white cotton bedsheets, comforter, and spreads. Her long silver hair was braided down her back; shorter strands and wisps curled around her face. She looked amazingly kempt for someone who had spent days in bed. And she did not look like someone who was about to die, I thought. She was gazing out the window at the sweeping landscape of this mountaintop estate. From her bedroom prospect, the view was all gently rolling green lawns sloping in gradually descending ridges, with the backdrop of the Southwest Mountains of Virginia rising beyond. In the morning light, pre-sunrise, the world was shades of spruce, indigo, and gray, deep dark hues waiting for the sun. I was now studying the view from the window with her.

It was spectacular and unusually devoid of fog today. How often had I forgotten to look at this sublime setting and pause to reflect on its silent beauty? I couldn't imagine what was going on in Ms. Bernadette's mind. I broke my reverie first, as duty called. Members of my family had long been employed at Ferncliff Estate. Our generations before were enslaved. After the South lost the war, my family and others were deeded land in the valley and, over the years, came to inhabit pocket-size towns and hollows that sprung up in the nooks and crannies of the Southwest Mountains. Through the generations, many in my family worked for the Estate, even with the changing of family ownerships.

I first came as apprentice to my mother, who was the lead housekeeper at the time, but it wasn't long before Ms. Bernadette asked for me as her personal assistant. My wages were minimal in the beginning since I was a minor and an apprentice and were given to my mother. When I turned eighteen, my mother and the estate changed my work status to full time with benefits. I had finished my high school education by correspondence school, studying at night and mailing my work to the school headquarters in Maryland. However, I did not intend to continue being a housekeeper indefinitely, and planned on saving up to move to Washington D.C. in a year or so. The idea inspired me everyday, as living in the city seemed so much more exciting than the quiet and slow-pace of life in the valley and in Mountains. Ms. Bernadette kept a rather distant awareness of my personal life, but in a tacit way, she supported me by rarely interfering on my personal time or obstructing my occasional need to go on leave from the estate.

"Well, Ms. Bernadette, shall I have Shamus fix you some breakfast?"

"Why yes, that would be splendid. And I would like to dress today." Then she stated what had been obvious, "Apparently, the angel of heaven is not coming for me after all."

"No, ma'am." I smiled.

"Well then, we have much to do."

A breakfast tray was ordered, the commode pot taken away, day clothes selected, and then there was the matter of the red carpet stain.

"Ms. Bernadette? Have you any idea what occurred here on this carpet? I don't remember seeing this stain yesterday."

My mistress raised an eyebrow. "What stain? What are you talking about?" She started to rouse herself from the bed. I assisted her over to the scene of the crime, and she peered at it with astonishment. Now I knew Ms. B.'s family roots were not Southern, but I supposed she lived in these parts and around us long enough to adopt some of our ways. "My lands, child, what in the tarnation happened here?"

I knelt at the stain, which spanned about fifteen inches, to inspect it more closely. It seemed dry, and my best guess would name it as red wine, although a vigorous balsamic vinegar would create the same effect. Or blood.

"That is unacceptable!" she started to say, but then her voice trailed off, and she grew quiet as she stared at it, and I could tell her mind was busy looking for a clue, a hint of some kind. I waited. All at once, I could see us both standing there in that magnificent old world bedroom of mahogany and upholstered furniture, heavy brocade drapes, Persian carpets, glass lamps and marble-topped side tables, the wardrobe, the vanity, the heavy carved door and ancient wall art, paintings, and sketches in guilt frames. She, the wingless white angel, crinkled with age after spending too many years on top of the Christmas tree, and me, the dark young woman with café au lait smooth skin, braided hair bundled beneath my scarf, rough in hand, and strong in body—standing together.

For a moment, I was swirling with déjà vu, a feeling of instant recognition and familiarity that all this already happened before: our two souls standing together in a magnificent room, peering at a bowl of blood. I thought it was blood, but now I was not sure. A dense liquid, or maybe it was just dark in color. We were both distressed.

Ms. Bernadette was bending at the waist over the Persian carpet to get a better look. I instinctively put a hand near her back in preparation to support her. "That looks like blood! Did someone slaughter a small animal in here?" As she straightened back up, I was the one who felt like I might need a steadying hand, the effects of the déjà vu still tingling in my head and stomach.

Ms. B. stepped lightly over to her reading chair and sat, lifting the folds of her nightgown and placing her feet on the brocaded footstool; the look on her face was deep in thought. I reached for the bedpost to steady myself, my own mind trying to engage with my thoughts while the images of what I had just seen both here in the room and in that great hall continued to merge and play together.

"Have Shamus clean this up as soon as possible."

"But, ma'am, don't you want to find out what happened?" I had steadied myself to regain my faculties; after all, I was at work, and falling into déjà vu was not part of my job description. The look she gave me was swift and precise and was intended to stop all further questioning, which it did. Just then, Shamus himself entered with the breakfast tray, which was highly unusual.

"Good mornin', my lady," he said as he entered, his eyes rapidly taking in the tableau of the room and its occupants. "I see I brought the wrong tray. You are already out of bed." He went to the small round table by the arched window and settled the contents of the breakfast tray in an inviting array on the white tablecloth, including a small crystal bud vase containing a single pink rose. He then stood

5

to the side of the table and made a sweeping gesture with his hand. "Madame." He glanced at me, bowed to her, and left the room.

I went to Ms. B. and walked her to the breakfast table. She brushed me away as she sat.

"I guess Shamus didn't notice the stain of the carpet," I said, starting to feel like something strange was seeping out of a box and filling the room, and no one was saying anything.

"Hmmmm" was all she said and busied herself with maneuvering all the fine dining accessories this household seemed intent on still using to consume simple food. More out of anger than obedience, I went after Shamus and saw his back disappear through the doorway to the downstairs kitchen.

Shamus had arrived from Scotland to Ferncliff Estate a few years ago during an unusually turbulent turnover of household staff and assumed the vacated head cook position in a very businesslike manner. The previous head cook, Mrs. Dample, who had been at Ferncliff for decades, had reached a point of decline to which even those of us loyal to employment had to concede she and her food were crumbling.

Shamus remained a mystery to most of us, not only as an outsider but also because of his very private nature. His food and work seemed to please Ms. Bernadette, however, and we all soon learned to accept his presence on the team.

"Excuse me, Shamus!" I entered the kitchen, and he turned from the stove.

"Yes, miss?" His face was positively neutral; his eyes were looking at me but with a blank expression. Something about his walled-off effect briefly stopped me in my thoughts. "Can I help you?"

"Yes. The carpet. In Ms. Bernadette's room. There's a huge bloodstain on it."

"A bloodstain? My, my. And how might I be helpful?"

"Well, Ms. Bernadette specifically said to me to have you clean it up." As soon as the words came out of my mouth, I realized how ludicrous it sounded. I knew as well as anyone that Shamus did not perform housekeeping duties. I realized I was digging myself into an interpersonal quicksand and decided not to say anything more for fear of throwing not only myself but also Ms. B. under the bus. "Never mind, sir. I'll find housekeeping."

"That's better," he replied lightly, his Scottish accent adding a stinging lilt to end this awkward encounter. He resumed his activity at the stove, and I went out to find Betsy.

Betsy was my friend. She was hired on at Ferncliff last year and was finishing her apprenticeship in housekeeping. She was no-nonsense, brisk, and hardworking, the right fit for her job. Mrs. Rutledge, head housekeeper, was determined to mold Betsy into the ranks of eventual leadership in the household, if that's what Betsy wanted. Betsy could excel at whatever she did, so I think the senior staff was curiously watching her unfold.

Betsy carried her caddy of cleaning supplies. "Blood, you think?"

"Not sure, but well, you'll see." I entered the bedroom first and put a hand out to stop Betsy outside the door. "Give us a few minutes." Ms. Bernadette had taken up trying to dress herself in an oversize floral caftan, which was not the ensemble we picked out earlier.

"I'm going outside to the garden. Where are my galoshes?"

I had to think for a moment and then remembered them amid her riding clothes in the dressing closet. "Ma'am, Betsy is here to clean the carpet stain."

"Leave it for now." Instructions were changing so fast this morning I wanted to clarify.

"Leave it, just for now, as in not today?"

Ms. Bernadette suddenly focused her eyes on me. I assumed my waiting stance. I had learned the importance of asking one question at a time rather than responding immediately to every new direction. For a moment, time stood still. I could see us there as if looking down on the scene: Betsy paused outside the bedroom door with her cleaning caddy slung on her arm, leaning in slightly to hear us, and me standing halfway between the dressing closet and Ms. Bernadette, who was now tented in a large loose floral dress, her bare feet peeking out from underneath, waiting on the galoshes. It was becoming a strange day.

"There's something I must see in the garden that may explain that stain," she said, seemingly perking up more and more by the minute.

I informed Betsy to wait on cleaning the stain. We both knew she'd examine it for curiosity's sake when the room was vacant. I helped Ms. B. into her galoshes, grabbed her walking cane with the ivory and mother-of-pearl handle, and we set out for the garden.

CHAPTER 2

I ANTICIPATED THIS WOULD be a long walk for Ms. Bernadette today as she had been in bed for so long. I suggested we exit through the solarium, which would take us through the greenhouse and, in turn, set us out into the flower gardens with the woods beyond. Ms. B. walked at a slow but steady pace; I trailed closely behind. She greeted every staff member we passed, and they gave her a cheery hello, a good morning, a nice to see you out, and about. I smiled at everyone and answered a few quizzical looks with an "All is well" nod. The staff was aware of Ms. Bernadette's rather long spell of not feeling well and her subsequent withdrawal to her room.

The garden in summer was a cheerful display of bright color, with brown-eyed Susans, petunias, roses, gerber daisies, and lamb's-ear. Mason and Rebecca were already hard at work with wheelbarrow, shovel, bags of fertilizer, clippers, and straw hats. They waved at us, looking somewhat curious to see Ms. Bernadette in the garden so early in the day. She occasionally would come out with the clipping basket to make a bouquet or two, which the staff would then feature prominently in the foyer. Ms. B. had lived at this estate since she was a child. I was still learning bits and pieces of her past to add to the formal knowledge imparted by my mother. Ms. B. had lived abroad several times in Europe and wanted to remain in Scotland at one time, but her husband demanded her to return home.

It was the lingonberry patch she went to this morning, situated at the edge of the garden not far from the wooded area. The lingonberry grew with other berry bushes, planted intentionally for household use. The red lingonberry was rather bitter and made into jelly, added to marmalade for Christmas, and even drank as a tonic by Ms. B. I never thought much about it. Today, however, the bright red juicy berries practically thrummed with guilt as we approached them; my thoughts returned to the dramatic stain on the carpet. The sun was already warming up the morning, and I could see a sheen of perspiration on Ms. B.'s forehead. *Oh dear. The walk to the garden is too arduous for her first time out since the deathbed saga,* I thought. I stood beside her as we peered at the shrubs.

"OK, so who would do this, and why?" I said, forgetting for a moment my place and starting to relish the role of detective. I glanced at her as she did not respond. She seemed deep in thought. I was not even sure she heard my question. The memory of the déjà vu experience came back to me, and in this moment of silence, I had time to give it more thought. Like a dream, the images were already faded, but I know the "scene" included Ms. B. and myself except we were in another time and place. It seemed medieval and European. I knew I needed to intentionally stash the details in my mind before they disappeared forever. Scotland popped into my head next, so before I could doubt myself, I locked that detail down too.

A voice suddenly called out clear and distinct as day: "We need your help!" I looked from the lingonberry and searched around me. It wasn't Ms. B.; she was fine, standing still, as if she never heard anything. I turned toward Mason and Rebecca to see what they needed, but they were hard at work, bent over the soil. Now I spun the rest of the 180 degrees to see who called, and there was no one. My movement roused Ms. B.

"What is it, child?"

"Did you hear that voice?"

"You heard a voice?"

"Yes, calling for help, but I don't see anyone." She immediately looked over toward the woods and gestured with her finger. Right. Of course. Why didn't I think of that? "I'll go check it out," I said.

"Wait, I'm coming too," replied Ms. B.

I hesitated. "You better wait here."

"No, I'm coming. I've got my galoshes on. Go on, I'll follow you. I'll catch up."

I knew not to argue with her. She was beaming, her cheeks were flushed in a healthy pink, her eyes were dancing and alive, maybe the walking was good for her. She seemed OK.

We walked into the woods together.

A Virginia woods on a summer day is a beautiful thing indeed. A well-worn footpath of dirt, leaves, and small pebbles guided us through an opening in the tree line. Just a few steps in and already, the outside world was receding in scope and memory. The dense canopy of foliage from maple, oak, black walnut, hickory, and pine created a sanctuary of cool shade and oxygen-rich air that began to infuse my lungs with energy. I instinctively took some deep breaths and slowed my breathing.

Ms. Bernadette behind me paused, and I turned around and said, "I don't see anyone."

"Call out," she responded.

I raised my voice and projected into the trees. "Hello, is anyone there?"

We waited and not a sound except the cicadas starting up their daily drone and a slight rustle of leaves on the ground from the movement of small creatures. Otherwise, the stillness was palpable. The morning light in the woods was shady and blue, with the occasional scrim of pale sunlight beaming through the trees.

"Hello, is anyone there?" I called again, with still no response.

We walked a few more paces, the path rounding the trunk of a very old hickory. I felt and saw swift movement ahead between the forked trunk of the next tree. I halted suddenly, and Ms. B. did too, nearly colliding into me.

"Hello, somebody? We are here to help."

I knew we were closer now to whoever might have called to me earlier, and I did not sense malevolence. I walked to the tree with the twin trunks in the shape of a *V* and peered through, freezing suddenly. I was eye to eye with a child-sized person clinging to the back side of the tree trunk with all fours, like a koala bear hugs a tree limb. The little person's appearance was astonishing, my mind trying to make sense of what I was seeing. Though small in size as a five- or six-year-old, this person was much older in age, with a wizened face full of creases and brown as a nut, with a thatch of dark curly hair and attired in what appeared to be camouflage garb of fur, feathers, and leaves.

"Hello. Are you hurt?" I blurted out. Just then, Ms. B. came around the other side of the tree and stood stock-still, gazing at the little person, who was loosening his grip on the tree and starting to descend to the ground. I walked around the tree too and crouched to my knees, so I was at eye level to our new acquaintance. "My name is Eva."

"And I'm Lady Bernadette," I heard Ms. B. say, and I cinched my eyebrows for a moment, struck by the added title she gave her name. The little person placed a hand over its heart and bowed slightly to us both.

"I am called Dabbs," he said in a throaty, deep voice. He fixed his gaze on Ms. B. "I was sent to find you, my lady. We are in need of human guidance in my realm."

A distinct breeze lifted through the woods at that moment. I shifted to my other knee and waited, for this was not my conversation anymore, even though I had loads of questions for both parties.

Ms. B. leaned hard on her cane and set her penetrating gaze on Mr. Dabbs. "I can see this journey was hard on you. As a matter of fact, I do not convene with your realm anymore. Not since Rathven. How did you find me?"

Dabbs glanced at me. "Sinnott found your beacon, my lady."

"My beacon! What do you mean . . ." And she turned to look at me, and her face darkened. "Eva, what do you know? How can this be? What have you not told me?"

12

Good lord, I did not expect to be yanked into this already strange encounter. "I truly am as surprised as you, ma'am. I don't know what you both are talking about, I don't know who Sinnott is, and what are these other realms?"

Both Dabbs and Ms. B. moved closer to me. I was feeling quite uncomfortable. "YOU heard the voice calling for help. I did not. YOU showed me the stain on the carpet." Ms. B. paused, and I just remained mute, completely unsure what to say. Mr. Dabbs started to fidget, and Ms. B. closed her eyes.

"Eva, if you were some kind of beacon to the realm Dabbs speaks of, well, I can tell you are unaware." She began to look weary and needed to sit and shuffled her way over to a fallen log. I immediately went to help her, fully capable of performing my assistant role at least. I glanced back at Dabbs, who watched us curiously. He ambled over to us.

"My lady and miss, the invitation I bring from Demistrath is for you to attend the Wisdom Circle at Lughnasadh. Dev Sinnott has asked for you. I am here to escort you." Mr. Dabbs stood earnestly in front of Ms. B., and I was struck by his sincerity, his invitation to another realm called Demistrath notwithstanding.

Ms. Bernadette spoke. "Lughnasadh is August 1. I would have to find a reason, a ruse to be away. I would have to bring Eva. She attends me. I did not expect to return to Demistrath, Mr. Dabbs. You can tell this Dev Sinnott this is quite unordinary. And it has been years, decades even, since I have stepped foot there. My health fails and returns. Not long ago, I thought I was on my deathbed. And then there is the matter of my husband to contend with. He hates it when I go away."

"I will relay the message, my lady. Sinnott suggested the escort start from Warm Springs. Can you arrange it?"

Ms. B. perked up and beamed at me. "A trip to Warm Springs is a splendid idea!"

Our expedition to Warm Springs and the mysterious rendezvous point with Dabbs was quickly arranged. Ms. Bernadette was not a demanding employer and typically followed a quiet, genteel sort of routine. So when she asked for something specific, the staff fell into a regimental response with precision and thoroughness to rival a British Royal household, I would imagine. The car and chauffeur were made ready; I was to go along to attend to her, and oddly, she asked Shamus to come too, which would leave Ferncliff without a head cook, but he accepted his command without a lift in the brow and began packing a pantry of food for a few days. The ruse Ms. B. perpetrated for the trip was the need to "take to the baths" to cleanse herself after her deathbed illness.

Mr. Dabbs had left us in the woods, practically vanishing behind the split tree trunk. I surged to go see where he went, but Ms. B. pulled me homeward. "Never mind, Eva. He's gone already. You'll see plenty of this, and more, when we are in Demistrath." She spoke so matter-of-factly as if she were telling me about all the sweets I would find in a bakery. My curiosity ran strong, and there was a part of my brain that reacted with ease and familiarity to these unusual events. In a way, I trusted Ms. Bernadette. Her willingness to fold me into her private life proved a trust I gave her as my boss and respected elder.

On our walk back to the house after Mr. Dabbs departed, she told me several things that solidified my curiosity and loyalty. She explained that we could not talk of these woodland matters in the house. "There are too many people who know nothing about these realms, these histories, these legacies. I have learned to stay silent because I have been hospitalized before, a long time ago, for being too frank about my experiences."

She went on to explain how the carpet stain was actually a secret distress symbol established from her Rathven days, something she had not thought about for many years, but once she realized it was not wine or blood, the lingonberry became the apparent clue. "When I went to Rathven, the fairy folk . . . I'm sorry, Eva. I must sound like a crazy person. There's too much to tell you right now. In time, child. In time."

After Betsy was bidden to clean the stain, she confirmed to me it was not blood, but she couldn't get the stain out. She went on to add that the word among staff was Shamus must have included the berries on a meal tray at Ms. Bernadette's request. I knew that explanation was farfetched, but there were more prominent things to focus on now, and a wave of heaviness overcame me, knowing I had started a chain of keeping secrets from my best friend.

CHAPTER 3

W E LEFT THE estate on the morning of August 1 for the two-hour drive to Warm Springs. I sat in the back seat with Ms. B., and Shamus rode up front with the driver, Hans. The trunk of the Buick Riviera was packed to the brim with the effects for the three-day getaway. I felt quite excited.

The Warm Springs bathhouses were primitive at best. They were a pair of round wooden structures with peeling white paint and grooved lumber planks and looked as if no one had updated them since they were built. I was a bit surprised. Inside, the spring-fed pools remained a constant temperature of ninety-eight degrees, and the bathing pool areas were lined with rocks, and the floor of the pools were pebbles. The water was about four to five feet deep, and the round wooden bathhouses were built around and over these pools, with an interior boardwalk that circled the entire perimeter of the pool.

Sectioned off like slices of pie from the center pool were individual changing rooms, and a plastic shower curtain closed off each room for privacy. In each changing room was a single wood or wicker stool, an 8 x 10 framed mirror hanging on a wall post with a wire, and several wire hooks for draping one's towel or clothes. The floorboards had gaps in places between them with vague glimpses of stone and the murmur of running water beneath. "The bathhouses were erected in

1761 and 1836, and they were quite the draw from around the state for refreshing, convalescing, and improving one's health.

There was a town of Warm Springs, Virginia, a small grotto of clapboard cottages. Our car pulled up to the old millhouse, now renovated as an inn. Our driver, Mr. Hans, checked us in, while Shamus paced outside the car smoking a cigarette, his footsteps crunching on the gravel as Hans came out, and they began to unload Ms. B. and the luggage. We were escorted to a small two-bedroom suite joined by a cozy sitting area with a fireside hearth. The men were in a separate room that had a kitchenette.

"Lunch will be served presently. Would you like to be indoors or out on the patio?"

Shamus had knocked on our door after I helped Ms. B. out of her travel shoes and into house slippers. We dined on the patio, in warm sun, but with the shade of a striped awning strung from the French doors and extended to a nearby tree. I assisted Ms. B. with her lunch while nibbling on my own plate of sandwich, grapes, and cheese slices. I started to wonder when, where, and how we would arrange a secret rendezvous with the woodland people while going about in such a constant state of public routine. But Ms. B. had it all figured out. After a short nap, we would "take to the baths." Then a light early dinner, after which the men were excused to the local pub for the evening, Ms. B. being ready for bed from all the fresh air and warm mineral baths.

"You are both off duty until breakfast, but I expect my coffee at 7:00 a.m."

The afternoon soak in the warm water was indeed very relaxing. We were dropped off at the women's house, and men bathed in the other house, a short jaunt down the lane. I helped Ms. B. into her bathing suit and water shoes. She lowered herself into the water from the wooden steps, with me close behind. There were small white Styrofoam boards bathers could bob around with, and Ms. B. seemed to enjoy that. I looked up at the vaulted round ceiling with a round skylight open to the natural air that beamed down into the pool.

We practically had the pool to ourselves as the summer months are not a big draw for warmwater bathing. The attendant was out of sight in her little office, the sound of an electric fan whirling contentedly. Ms. B. told me how she came to these pools in her childhood and how well she knew the area. "There's a wooded grove not from our inn we can walk to this evening. That's where we'll meet Mr. Dabbs." And while we bobbed around in the warm spring water, Ms. Bernadette told me more of her life story.

She was born in France in 1915, and her father, a low-level diplomat with a pronounced interest in Spiritualism and Theosophy, came to America with his family, where they lived in Virginia. Ms. B.'s father acquired Ferncliff Estate in a closed-door postwar dealing to this day she didn't fully understand. She was an only child and remembered the foreign service life from the domestic standpoint: sheltered from American public culture, privately tutored through high school, and frequently exposed to the private dinner parties her parents hosted, both the political ones and the personal ones. The latter were focused on discussion groups and book readings on early New Age topics like spirit guides, angels, clairvoyants, astrology, and ancient oracle tools.

"It wasn't until I was a teen that I fully learned my parents' spiritualism was not readily accepted by mainstream society. When I went off to Mary Baldwin College, I spent those years trying to fit in with my American classmates, and I drifted away from my parents' quirky after-work soirees. My mother, in particular, enjoyed all the Epicurean delights and would bring me along when I was a child with her society wives to the Warm Springs and also to the Homestead Resort, a more lavish hotel in Hot Springs just up the road. It was here in Warm Springs, during my many solitary walks in the woods, that I first met the woodland folk. It wasn't Mr. Dabbs but a younger sprite and nymph, a pair, that would find me, and we'd converse and play for hours in a space between our two worlds. It was a small glade where the energy and air would distinctly change—it's hard to describe—part vibration, part tingle, part like water around your body when you stand in the sea. They asked me lots of questions about my world and giggled a lot. He was called Festus, and she was named Astrid. One day they even invited me to their realm. I was young, so I didn't stop to question how that would be possible. Children are much more in tune with the metaphysical side of things."

I listened to Ms. B. with intrigue and wonder. Her life was the stuff of novels I read; little did anyone know this petite silver-haired aristocrat had so many unusual experiences. Had I not seen Mr. Dabbs myself, I would have doubted Ms. B., but he was as real in that woods as any living being, and this evening, he would meet us again, and we would go to their Wisdom Circle, in another realm. For the first time in this whole sequence of events, I felt my belly clutch with a pang of fear. My wits began to scold me to come to my senses.

"But I am completely in my senses," I retorted to the frightened voice inside me. "Besides, I'm on duty here, and my job is to attend to Ms. B. She said so herself. I must move forward with this plan." Truth be told, my curiosity won out over my fear.

Back at the Mill House Inn, the summer afternoon was descending into the hills and valleys, casting interesting shadows of distinct geometric angles throughout the landscape. I felt a tingle of a breeze penetrate my skin, nudging the coils of hair at my neck. I was wearing my staff uniform, a light blue sheath dress with short sleeves and a collar, buttons down the front, and a cloth belt. Black Mary Jane shoes and, in the summertime, no pantyhose, thank goodness. We all wore small pin-on name badges that read Ferncliff Estate in letterhead and our first name in larger print. Mr. Hans had a vest with the Ferncliff Estate logo embroidered on it. Shamus, well, he did not wear identifiable garb of the estate, which only confirmed my increasing hunch that he was a personal friend of Ms. B. and was hiding out in this job as some sort of cover for a secret past. Now where I got that idea, I didn't know. My imagination was constantly feeding me extra ideas that always kept me entertained or amused.

I dressed in my own clothes for our walk to the woods after dinner. Ms. B. was using her cane more for balance than support. Her gait was steady and purposeful. There was nothing unusual about this early evening stroll across the lawn, two people enjoying a midsummer evening. I had looked up in my dictionary the word "Lughnasadh" and discovered it was one of the eight seasonal sacred days celebrated by pagan people in Europe in honor of the first harvest. It represents protection, luck, abundance, and healing. It is also spelled "Lughnasa," which fits our version of phonetics a little better, I guess.

I was struck by the word "pagan" since all we heard about pagan people was negative, usually referencing godless unbelievers, even Satan worshippers. Goodness, that didn't seem right! So again, the dictionary revealed that "paganism" is an umbrella term covering a variety of nature-based and polytheistic religious systems that have been around for millennia, long before the Christian era, and got bumped off the platform of major world religions because of the lack of a strong male leader whom followers could organize around and worship. Pagans rallied instead around Mother Earth and remained connected to nature, and paganism was practiced indigenously all over the world.

I was curious and eager to meet the woodland people tonight and wondered what kind of distress they were in that required the attendance of Ms. Bernadette.

She now paused at the edge of the woods and surprised me by grabbing my hand. Gripping firmly, she spoke. "May that which transpires here be for the good of all."

It sounded like a prayer to me, so I said, "Amen." She smiled briefly, dropped my hand, and we walked into the woods together.

CHAPTER 4

T HIS PATCH OF woods seemed more delicate to me. The tree trunks were thinner and spaced further apart from one another. From the ground protruded more bushes and shrubs, the kind that flower in the spring; there was no particular path to follow, and my ear caught the sound of trickling water. Ferns embanked a small stream that meandered through the woods, a fallen log or two intermittently landing here and there. An early evening hush fell upon the woods at this time of day as birds quieted down for the night, and squirrels were wrapping up their daytime marathon of foraging. Insects remained present in the summer, and I was cognizant of a few mosquito drones and had to flick away gnats. The air was still and humid but not too hot. As we approached the fallen log, I noticed a perimeter of small stones was intentionally laid out in a giant circle on the ground, encompassing the log, and a heap of charred sticks and kindling that looked like remnants of a fire. Really? Fire in the woods? The stream gurgled nearby.

Ms. B. stepped into the stone ring and motioned me to follow. We sat ourselves down on the log to wait. After a few moments, she stood with a chuckle.

"It's been so long since I've done this. I forgot I need to call on them." She stood and relaxed her arms by her sides. She took a couple of deep breaths, rubbed her palms together, and then raised her arms on either side of her like wings, palms up.

"I call on the overlighting deva of nature. I call on the sacred spirit of Gaia. Make a door to Demistrath."

I sat expectantly, not sure where to look or what would happen. Ms. B. kept her eyes closed and arms raised and then slowly lowered her arms.

Mr. Dabbs was sitting beside me on the log. The phrase "out of nowhere" was the best way I could say it. No sound, no shift in the air, no light changes or temperature changes. Just there he was, warm, smelly, hairy, leafy, still in a somber mood. He nodded to me, and Ms. B. turned around.

"The Wisdom Council awaits you, my lady. But I must warn you. Dev Sinnott is in a rare mood. Ever since Queen Merideth expired, Dev Sinnott has, well, taken over."

"Taken over? How can that be? What of the new queen?"

"Well, that's just the thing, madame. We have no queen." Dabbs paused as the look on Ms. B.'s face went from confusion to consternation. She began to pace, and I jumped to be near her.

"The council suggested your invitation, under the guise you bring the human experience of mastering the season of perpetual harvest. Dev Sinnott believes you could be helpful to his goals for Demistrath. He remembers you were at Rathven and assumes you have the secret human science that allows modern man to dominate the earth, which is what he is seeking at this time."

"But, Mr. Dabbs, none of this is true. You know that. Look at me, I am an old woman. I can't stop a despot."

Mr. Dabbs stood patiently. "My lady, where I come from, you are only beginning to reach your prime. Please help us. The council pleads. We all need you." Then he stopped and looked down. Suddenly, he looked squarely at me. "And you."

Ms. B. and I stared at each other. This invitation had moved far beyond a friendly visit. I could tell by her face she had many questions as did I, of course.

"Eva, I must ask you. Given all the unknowns, are you willing to go with me? You don't have to."

I found myself releasing a long exhale. I remembered a conversation with Mason and Rebecca about the commitments we make and how there is a point of no return where one realizes there is no choice but to forge on. To go back would be more dangerous to the soul than to keep moving forward. In some reality, I suppose I could have said, "OK, I'll wait here for you." Actually, that would have been rational. If all this mystical fantasy was just her imagination and in her mind, and she "went there," the worse that could happen was she'd keel over in the woods, and I'd run for help. Truth is, I was seeing the imaginary world too, in the very real form of Mr. Dabbs.

It was then the air changed, and a light gusty breeze began to stir in the woods, moving the branches and leaves in different directions.

"I'm going," I said to my two companions.

Mr. Dabbs wasted no more time and grabbed a hand of both of us and led us to the center of the circle, where the charred sticks lay.

"Step right on top of them," he said as he led the way.

We huddled together, feeling the crunch and snap of twigs beneath our shoes. I wanted to keep my eyes open, but a force beyond reckoning pervaded, and the scene went dark. I could still feel the grasp of Ms. B. and Dabbs, but a centrifugal force was moving all my internal organs and flesh in a distinct thrust down. The best I could compare it was to the start or end of a rollercoaster ride.

Everything went silent. A stillness returned to our bodies. I opened my eyes as Mr. Dabbs gently pulled us apart. We were standing in green grass on a sloping hillside overlooking an open valley, cut through by a river, with clusters of homes built of rock and timber on either side. A single stone bridge connected both sides of the village, and several small dinghies were tethered to a wooden pier that jutted out from a stone plaza I guessed was the marketplace. At this time of day, it was quiet and empty. We seemed to be in the same time zone and latitude as Virginia, but the cluster of homes and time era had old Europe all over it.

"Where are we, Mr. Dabbs?"

"This is Demistrath, in the county Terragon. But for now, I must take you to the council, up on the hill here." He gestured upward, glancing with concern at Ms. B., who had already commenced forward in a sturdy, purposeful march up the grassy slope. A small black animal was making its way toward us from the top of the hill; I could tell by its movements it was a cat, which soon reached us and mingled among the three of us as we ascended to the crest.

The scene before us was both familiar and fantastic. The council had gathered within a circle of boulders and slabs of stone, some members sitting, some standing. Center circle, a fire burned in a steel half drum, tended by a young person who seemed to be the same dwarf/elf species as Mr. Dabbs. The sun was beginning its gradual descent behind the circle, where another valley lay beyond, making this hilltop a spectacular place to see multiple views.

We stopped at the entrance to the stone circle, and all eyes moved toward us and became still. The black cat was the only thing that moved as it angled deliberately over to a tall standing figure in full hooded Druid robe. More than a dozen other people had gathered to surround the fire cauldron, arranged in various distances from the fire, some closer, some farther away, dressed in swaths of fabric, leather, hides, vines, and straw clothing assembled in ways we might only see at Halloween or some fantastical costume parade.

Mr. Dabbs stepped forward. "Our guests have arrived—Lady of Ferncliff and young Lady Eva."

He bowed toward Sinnott and then stepped to the side. A small woman close to the entrance stood and stepped toward us, reaching out her hands, and grabbed the hand of Ms. Bernadette.

"Bernadette, it is I, Astrid!" she whispered as she ushered her to a place in the circle.

I followed. Astrid, the fairy playmate I had just heard about in Warm Springs! My head was starting to spin a little more. The need to whisper was worrisome, and I glanced over at the tall hooded specter I assumed was Dev Sinnott. I wasn't sure if Dev was a title or his first name. No one was speaking.

Astrid stood about four feet tall and had a regal bearing, with gold and silver hair gathered in mounds on her head held in place by a tiara of vines, leaves, flowers, and feathers. She placed Ms. B. on an upturned tree stump, and I stood behind but within arm's reach. Astrid glanced back at me, and for a moment, our eyes locked. There was a concern in her eyes but also a dancing curiosity. I liked her immediately. The juxtaposition of Astrid's energy and that of the cloaked dark cloud that was Mr. Sinnott was beginning to give me a headache. I started to pick up the energies of the others around the circle; there were fear, loathing, boredom, anger, confusion, and nausea. I could feel Mr. Dabbs behind me somewhere; his now familiar vibration was steadfast determination, laced with kindness and patience.

I realized I felt a love for him already as I sorted through all the emotions now swirling around me. The energy in this circle was becoming turbulent, and I felt dizzy. I sat on the grass, hoping not to draw attention to myself, pushing my hands into the grass and poking my fingertips into the dark soil. Immediately, I began to feel better.

CHAPTER 5

D EV SINNOTT HAD begun to speak, and all the throbbing energies I had felt from the council were now suspended in bated stillness.

"This council shall now commence. Roll call has been taken. We have noted the presence of two visitors. Their late arrival has delayed us. We will move forward to align with the setting sun."

He turned and faced the sunset, his arms stretched out wide, and the council members all shifted to face west, standing as well and raising their arms to salute the sun.

I merely watched, aware of both my outsiderness and my hesitation, not willing to assume an action to which I had no introduction. Ms. B. appeared to half-heartedly join in, but she at least had some preexisting relationship with this world that I did not. I realized I was to be her bodyguard, a role that would allow me to be exactly what I wanted—the astute and vigilant observer.

The setting sun salute was done in silence and lasted a few minutes. Then they all turned back to the circle. Dev Sinnott continued, his voice was clear and strong, and although he remained hooded, I started to realize he might be younger than assumed.

"We gather on the first day of the month of the corn moon, Lughnasa, as our ancestors called it. Season of harvest. A time to consume all that the earth has given us, to harness the power of abundance. In Demistrath, we have toiled for centuries with backbreaking work to prepare for the long winter survival. We have remained frozen in time with this primitive way of life, year after year, in a pattern of assumption and ignorance which has become ridiculous.

"Our visitors come from a place that moved ahead with industry, harnessing science and new technology to take from the earth on their own terms and not to remain passively ruled by the whims and harsh ways of Mother Nature. You have suggested the Lady Bernadette to come here, and I have approved her visit based on the references of Astrid and Festus. But there is more you should know. You have heard of Rathven . . ." And here, Sinnott paused for dramatic effect, and on cue, the council began to murmur to one another in what mostly appeared to be indignation. Sinnott continued.

"It may surprise you to learn the lady here has been to Rathven and was part of that affront."

The council shifted wildly and focused on Ms. Bernadette, on us, I guess. A creeping unease flooded over me, and I stepped forward toward Ms. B. and blurted out, "What's this about?"

"Sshh, child, there are protocols . . ." Ms. B. sat remarkably stoic and put a hand out to me, moving to stand. "You confuse the council, Dev Sinnott. I was made to believe our invitation to this meeting was for a friendly collaboration. And now your reference to the Rathven endeavor has clearly caused alarm."

A wiry man with a gruff voice spoke up. "But is it true?" I could feel Mr. Dabbs behind us shift forward, stepping further into the circle."Dev Sinnott," Dabbs said, "might I suggest the council recess so that we may query our guests further? What you have said has caught some of us unawares, and before we continue, we would like to request the right to query our visitors."

A smirk plastered across the face of the hooded Sinnott. "As you wish, but you will not like what you learn. We are adjourned and will reconvene tomorrow."

Sinnott turned abruptly and strode away, followed by a trio of council members. The rest of the circle started to move away slowly, some hesitant, others confused or troubled, glancing at Ms. B., moving apart in silence. They headed down to the village. Mr. Dabbs, Astrid, and three other council members remained with us – a brunette woman named Lara, a man of small stature who I soon learned was Ms. Bernadette's other childhood friend, Festus, and the man who had confronted Ms. B. at the circle. The black cat had stationed itself on top of one of the rocks, within listening distance. Something told me to watch out for the cat. Something wasn't quite right there.

It was decided to go to the grotto, which apparently was the nearest home among this bewildered crew now awkwardly escorting us down the hill in the descending darkness. Lara scampered ahead and ushered us into a cramped and cozy kitchen. I noticed there were only four chairs around the table, so I stood behind Ms. B. After some nervous gesturing on who should take the seats, Festus and Mr. Dabbs remained standing. Mr. Dabbs began.

"My lady, I want to both apologize for troubling you and bringing you here. As you can see, our council has been struggling with the direction in which Sinnott has been steering us. He is the queen's son, and after our queen's unexpected passing, he stepped in during the funeral rites and started commanding ship. We had never paid him much mind. He was a sullen, lazy youth and for years had lived away from Demistrath. The queen rarely spoke of him, so little was he even in our awareness. When he returned to our village a couple of years ago, the queen set him up with some land for fielding, and again, no one thought much about him.

"Our queen was loved and esteemed, and she was gracious and strong, and our collective looked to her as our own facet of the goddess. She had brought to her tenure a resurgence of interest in the magic of nature. The council adopted seasonal celebrations and rituals that had been lost in practice over the past century, celebrating them in a new way, more festive and fun. The young ones in particular have reveled in the renaissance, and many are apprenticing in the crafts."

Astrid reached across the table and grasped Ms. B.'s hands. "My dear, it is so good to see you. This must all be so hard for you. I'm sorry I couldn't give you a proper welcome." She turned to our hostess. "Lara, do you have some tea? Lady Bernadette could use some tea."

"Oh my, where are my manners? Of course!" Lara sprang into action with a clang of pots and lids, running the water and igniting fire on the iron stove. I noticed no modern conveniences in this home; it was all very quaint and rustic.

"How long has Sinnott been the self-proclaimed king of the woods?" Ms. B. asked.

"For an annum, at least. His expectation that Demistrath is to move into the future similar to the humans is just preposterous, many of us think. Our realm is so much smaller and has always been agrarian and earth-based. In truth, we have been voyeurs in the human world, many of us gifted with dimensional crossovers, and we have watched the humans for millennia, not unlike you do in your movie houses. We watch, but we cannot have. Sinnott, we believe, has spent considerable time in the human world. He seems infected with another worldly view on things, but it is strange to us."

Astrid was interrupted with the arrival of teacups to the table and Lara pouring for everyone, pushing a jar of milk and a bowl of raw sugar toward the center of the table. Suddenly, the fourth and silent member of the council, and whom I almost forgot was present, spoke.

"With all due respect, there is the matter of Rathven we must discuss." Everyone turned to the wiry man who appeared middle-aged, lean, and gaunt, dressed in what I would call Germanic garb, leather lederhosen, shirt, vest, and wool Bavarian hat. "We need to hear from Lady Bernadette, to the charges of her ties to Rathven."

A sigh settled around the table. Mr. Dabbs was looking at me. "I can see you do not understand what Rathven is, Ms. Eva, and what it means to us. Rathven is a human settlement in Northern Scotland, where the members grow and raise gardens and plants of enormous size and abundance in a practically barren coastal area. It is said the leaders consort with the nature spirits firsthand to achieve this. Our feelings are that the nature spirits were colonized, if you will, for their magic to a point that was not mutually beneficial."

"Rathven is a spiritual commune, Eva." Ms. Bernadette looked at me. "The leaders professed close ties to the Christian god and proclaimed the success of their vegetable and plant gardens as a co-creation with God via these nature spirits. As you can imagine, this commune drew a wide group of spiritual seekers, quacks, skeptics, believers, and often very wounded people, similar to Catholic sightings of the Virgin Mary, now preserved as sacred places. I did go to Rathven when I was in my fifties. At the time, I was, well, many of those categories—seeker, wounded, searching for more meaning, I guess." She paused. The room was briefly silent.

Astrid spoke up. "Of course, you meant no harm, Bernadette. Dev Sinnott was unfair to bring up that information at the circle. Many on our council are not educated enough to discern what meaning to make of Sinnott's reference. All they know about Rathven is what Mr. Dabbs just now explained, and truthfully, we all feel the situation became harmful to the nature spirits, which, in turn, is an abuse of us in this realm. But Festus recounted to me that you tried to intervene on our behalf."

I was continually impressed with Astrid. She was loving and wise. "If I may ask a question, what happened to the nature spirits at Rathven?"

Astrid spoke again. "They died off, and the ones tied to us were the ones tied to Rathven. So you can see why Demistrath is afraid and angry about Rathven. When the nature spirits are eliminated, our ability to thrive is changed from joyful communion and collaboration with the earth to one of excessive toil and animosity. We have felt those effects more recently, and Dev Sinnott is not wrong in his awareness of this. However, his approach is one of unrestrained pushing into a future of modernizing, with science and technology, and we are not cut out for that. It will destroy us."

"So why send for me?" Ms. Bernadette sipped on her tea.

There was silence around the table. The Bavarian leaned into the table and pushed his tea away. "Lara, do you have anything stronger in your cupboard there?"

Astrid and Mr. Dabbs simultaneously spoke.

"This is probably enough for one night."

"I will escort you ladies back to your realm."

Ms. Bernadette didn't hesitate and gently set her cup down on the saucer. "I will leave. I thank you for your kind hospitality." She stood somewhat stiffly. I held her elbow. She started to shake me off, but then I felt her submit.

She and Astrid gave each other a rather awkward face kiss, and Mr. Dabbs was already leading the way out of the cottage.

The three of us stood outside in the cool night air. A vivid moon glowed in the dark sky, and a myriad of stars sparkled in their random array, constellations gently pulsing in silent rhythm like a heartbeat. I was mesmerized. Everything seemed so astounding it was hard to look away. In our world, the night sky seemed much farther away. Here, it fell like a curtain in arm's reach. I could feel my companions sharing the moment. Even Dabbs followed my gaze upward.

"It's so beautiful," I whispered.

"Aye, it is. But we must walk to the hill. Can you do it, Lady Bernadette?"

"I must, mustn't I? Unless you have a cart and horse?"

She sounded weary and irritated. *Oh dear. This adventure has taken its toll.*

"We will help you, not to worry," I said as cheerfully as I could, not wanting to look away from the stars. Mr. Dabbs and I each took an arm, and we stepped up the path to the hillside.

The trip back to Virginia was just as jolting as it was coming in. We apparated back in the woods, inside the stone circle.

Mr. Dabbs provided the farewell. "My ladies, it has been my privilege to escort you. I hope you can recuperate quickly." I felt him press a small object into my hand, and he spoke softly to me. "Use this to summon me. I am at your command." And with that, he was quite gone.

"Let's go get ourselves to bed, Ms. Bernadette."

Leaving the woods, we strolled at a slower pace back to the Mill House Inn. It was nighttime here too, but the air was muggy, and the sky was cloaked behind a mantle of gray clouds. The moon was nowhere to be seen. I found myself pining for Demistrath already.

CHAPTER 6

THE NEXT MORNING came sooner than I would have liked. The sun was up and flooding the dawn soon after six o'clock. When I smelled coffee wafting from the suite beside us, my mind left the cotton and fiber of my dreams, craning by eyes for one last look at the lingering images of the Demistrath council circled with the stones on the hilltop. *Was that real?* My mind quickly started to trip over itself as a flood of memories from the night before came pouring back. *Yes, my god, yes, it was real.* This propelled me upright in my bed and feet to the floor. I passed from my room to Ms. Bernadette's. She was still ensconced in her bedding, fast asleep. Yesterday's dimension travel must have taken a lot from her. I chided myself in a somewhat humorous way for thinking so easily of *inter-dimensional travel.*

"You have completely lost your marbles, Eva!" I said to myself.

I dressed back into my staff uniform, and while folding my clothes from last night, I found the small object Mr. Dabbs had given me. It was an amber quartz crystal pendant wrapped in copper wire with a bale for hanging. Strange. I remembered he whispered to use it to summon him. I was hesitant to rub it further, not knowing what that might do. I tucked it into the pocket of my jeans, unsure what else to do with it.

Coffee was calling. I tapped on the door to the kitchenette and heard footsteps coming to the door. Shamus opened the door and motioned me to enter. "How is the mistress?"

I replied, "Still sleeping." I followed him to the counter, and he poured a mug of coffee for me.

"Cream and sugar?" he said.

I replied, "Cream only."

After handing me my mug, he picked up the one he was drinking from. "And what does the madame have on her itinerary today?"

With Shamus, all his words sounded like birdsong, lilting and clipped, light and airy. I realized how little we had spoken with each other.

"I believe rest and another visit to the warm baths."

He had prepared a small buffet of breakfast items—muesli, fresh fruit, yogurt, crusty rolls, and cheeses. "Help yourself. Hans is still sleeping too. He knocked a few back last night." I selected some items on a plate. "Sit if you like, or the patio is open for business," Shamus said and then smiled. "Strange, isn't it, this little trip of hers?"

I was momentarily stunned by his friendliness. But my training quickly calculated for professionalism. "Thank you for the breakfast." I sat in the room, curious to see if there would be more conversation. "I guess I was a little surprised she wanted to hit the road so soon after her illness," I offered.

"But that's just it, isn't it? Was she really ill?" Shamus refilled his coffee.

I delayed my response for a sip of coffee and to finish chewing my food. He waited. Suddenly, the conversation had lurched into intimate disclosure about our employer, and coming from Shamus, who heretofore had been the epitome of stoic staff service, I became cautious.

"I believe she was, although we don't know with what. She slept all day, ate some." As I spoke, I remembered those days Ms. B. referred to as her deathbed. Most staff who had worked at Ferncliff Estate for a long time used the word "depressed." I had been assigned to sit in the room, mainly to keep an eye on her. I read many books and magazines and even sneaked some of my coursework in with me. Deciding to change the subject, I said, "And what are your plans for the day?"

"I am at the lady's service, of course! Meals to prepare, smokes to be enjoyed, books to read." He winked as he finished speaking, still gazing at me.

"Excuse me, I will go check on Ms. Bernadette."

Leaving my breakfast behind so I could open the door myself, I returned to our suite and locked the door quietly. *Whoa. That felt weird. I'm not sure I liked that friendly side of Shamus.* I stood by the French doors looking out to the patio and the lawn beyond. Seeing the woods off in the distance jolted me back to last night's event, and I was overcome by memories of Astrid, Dabbs, the black cat, Sinnott, the dimension travel, the starry night sky. I realized they all mattered to me more than I liked. I had to stop myself from imagining my return to Demistrath.

Girl, you might be going a little bit crazy, I thought, crossing my arms over my chest and rubbing my hands up and down my arms like I was cold.

A soft voice behind me said, "You're not crazy, Eva. It all happened."

I turned 180 degrees to see Ms. Bernadette standing in her white cotton nightgown, her bare feet silent on the carpet, her braided hair mussed and coming undone. She looked alert, and her blue eyes beamed. I wanted to run to her and hug her and ask her to tell me everything was going to be OK, hold me, and comfort me. Instead, I smiled and said, "Good morning. You must have been reading my mind."

Ms. B. smiled. "How did you sleep? I had quite a night. But first, I must dress, and coffee would be in order!" She padded over to the French doors and stood beside me. I didn't know if she spoke out loud, but I heard distinctly the words "We must be careful, you and I, for we have ventured upon a world in danger." There was a pause, and I strained in silence to hear more. I glanced at Ms. B., who was staring out into the expanse beyond the French doors.

I organized my thoughts in a brief silence and then purposefully thought this phrase: "We are to return and help them, right?" continuing to gaze outside as well.

Ms. B. stirred and let out a big sigh. A single word ricocheted through my being: "Yes."

This time I was looking at Ms. Bernadette, and I would swear on the good book her lips did not move. Her eyes met mine briefly and knowingly, and then she moved. This time she spoke aloud. "Help me dress, Eva. I want to picnic and read in the woods today. That stream has always been a favorite of mine."

After she was dressed and her hair redone, she asked to eat on the patio, so I helped her get seated outside. The morning daylight was perfect, just a little cooled off from the night before. The sun had brightened the sky, and the birds were chirping their morning twitters and calls. Shamus stepped onto the patio from the door of the kitchenette.

"Good morning, madame, miss." He came bearing a tray with mugs of steaming coffee and food from his buffet, setting it down on the patio table. He did not look at me and busied himself placing items in front of Ms. B.

"Good morning to you," she replied with enthusiasm. "I hope you boys had a good time last night."

"Aye, we did, madame. No worse for the wear."

"Good. Now could you please pack a picnic lunch for Eva and I? I want to read by the stream this morning, in the woods. Tell Hans to bring the folding chairs."

"Certainly, ma'am. Allow us to set it all up for you."

A hour later, we were walking down to the words, with picnic case in hand and the now hatted Ms. B. and her tote bag of books and newspaper. There was a bit of a tangle with the men, who insisted they carry everything down. Hans had gone ahead with chairs and a small TV tray for a table, while Shamus packed a picnic case. I assured them I could carry the picnic and thermos just fine, and Ms. B. confirmed our ability to "manage from here." I felt a little bad for them as they looked forlornly on as we strolled away, knowing they were not needed for the morning. Men were still having a very hard time letting women do any heavy lifting, I noticed, or at the least the ones who worked at Ferncliff Estate did.

We soon found our way to a wooded glade just beyond the stone circle and fallen log. I wondered if Hans saw the circle or if it held curiosity to other passersby. Ms. B. was humming a little tune as she situated herself into a striped folding beach chair and set some things on the table. I wondered how she could be so cheerful after our adventurous night.

"This is a perfect morning! I've been thinking a lot about what to do next, but I knew we had to get away from the others to talk with you about it. It's complicated, you know, keeping our experiences private from prying and curious eyes and ears.

"I don't know what you were taught to believe growing up, Eva, but I imagine it was a very limited worldview, that this planet was created by God in a burst of loneliness and that we are born, live, and then die and get sorted out in some afterlife."

I was listening raptly to her concise depiction. My community, of course, was a churchgoing one, and there was a good bit of praising God and coming to Jesus on Sundays, with a whole lot of love, hugs, and food. There was definitely a teaching message about a right way and a wrong way to live, and we better bet our safe bottoms to live the right way, but that was a bit tricky too, trying to figure it all out. We were taught the devil Satan was hard at work steering us off God's course, and his way was full of temptations and cravings for things we didn't have but wanted. Our jobs were to resist these temptations and live humbly and kindly. I didn't give it as much mind as some because my personal predilection was already to do what's right and follow what was laid out before me by my elders.

Now I understand many people are not so easy with the church way and struggle a lot, falling into the seven deadly sins—pride, greed, lust, envy, gluttony, wrath, and sloth. There was always a part of me curious about this side of life and not opposed to understanding the vices better so as to remain free of their hold. A college friend gave me a book that I read called *Zen and the Art of Motorcycle Maintenance*, which really blew my mind, but at the same time, I loved learning about this peaceful way of accepting everything life sent my way. The word for what I learned about was "metaphysics," thought over matter, contemplating our existence and understanding the side of life that cannot be seen, measured, or defined. This was all very exciting to me. But truly, I knew practically nothing about it.

I remembered yesterday in the Warm Springs bath house when Ms. B. was talking about her parents, she mentioned their spirituality, and I wanted to ask her more about that. It was not often I found people even mention some of those topics, much less have firsthand knowledge about it. Then last night, when I learned about Rathven in more detail and that Ms. B. had made a special trip there in the '60s seeking something, I wanted to learn more about that too. I was intrigued by world travel and exploration, having never done it.

I was soon pleased because as we settled into our chairs in the gentle woods of Bath County, Ms. B. told me her Rathven story. She said it was important for me to know more about it before we returned to Demistrath.

CHAPTER 7

THE VAUXHALL VIVA was speeding on A96 from Aberdeen, Scotland, to the village of Moray on a gray day in the summer of 1968. Bernadette Robinson, French American runaway from Virginia, was thinking what a bold and reckless thing she had done, and she knew Moncure would be trying to make sense of her letter and that it was cruel of her to leave him without notice. He was a proud traditional husband, and these "antics" of hers did not fit into his narrow and straight-laced way of life. They had been married already for thirty years, and it was in this year of their anniversary when Bernadette decided to bolt. She had planned and fantasized for years the myriad ways she could do this, and in the end, she settled for the runaway method rather than the harrowing and unpredictable "try to get permission" method. Men like Moncure would never understand this crazy, irrational need to abandon five decades of a tamed and scripted life that just seemed to march into the future with unchanging repetition. Her society friends would twitter and cluck about this rash, irresponsible choice. No one that she knew would approve or understand, and in the end, she turned away from the gilded cage of the life she lived, and like a wolf caught in the iron jagged jaws of an unseen trap, she gnawed off her leg to get free. "Who chooses to do that?" she asked herself over and over, and yet she never once thought of turning back. "I'm a mess," she said, shaking her head now as the Scottish countryside breezed through the open windows of her little rental car, the tails of her head scarf flapping contentedly around her neck.

Secretly, she was also proud of herself, for her courage to take her life into her own hands and strike out on a new course, following a new constellation of stars to a different future. Her fiftieth birthday had been more impactful that she imagined. She presumed it was a midlife crisis because her thoughts and ideas seemed to shape-shift into someone else's desires and perspective. It was like a sleeping giant inside her started to wake up, and she found herself drifting away from Ferncliff, from Moncure and the house staff and Virginia, and thinking more and more about places she still wanted to see and things she still wanted to do. Moncure had gifted her with a trip to France to visit her ancestral country, and perhaps that had started the stirring inside her. Or perhaps it was the invitation from a friend to accompany her to a special farm in Jeffersonton, Virginia, called Perelandra. Bernadette was captivated by the farm's circular organic gardens grown entirely in harmony with nature and the wisdom of nature spirits so that everything grew without pesticides, chemicals, or force. The founder and her team promoted this center for nature research, helping others improve their health, and the environment, and their lives.

Bernadette found herself dreaming more at night, wild and fantastical dreams full of mysterious places and images, and she started writing some of them in a dream journal, puzzled and intrigued by their encroachment. And then most bizarre of all, Bernadette was visited in a dream by Astrid and Festus. She shook her head thinking of them now, her imaginary playmates from the woods, appearing to her again in midlife, smiling and beckoning to her. The last dream contained a vivid image of Astrid flying toward Bernadette, coming up close face-to-face and whispering, "Find us."

That dream woke Bernadette, and she sat bolt upright with her heart beating faster. She remembered walking out to the woods that day, to the stone circle, where she often went to sit and think, or read, or write, and found herself waiting to see if Astrid and Festus would appear. "I'm losing my mind," she berated herself, but now months later, here she was, driving in Scotland to a place called Rathven in search of something mythical or magical or just plain exotic to contemplate.

"In all fairness," Bernadette told herself, "I come by this honestly, right, Mother? Father?"

She often spoke to her parents, both deceased, and missing them, especially now, in her fifty-third year, when she had gently but purposefully nudged her life to tumble off the shelf, not knowing where it would land. She wished she had paid more attention when she was young to their spiritualist activities because as they grew older, her parents seemed to fade away from those pursuits and became vague and foggy as they aged. So many questions she had for them now, but it was too late. As a youngster, she never cared for or appreciated their spiritual interests and, consequently, did not get to know that side of her parents. Unless those practices are taught down through the generations, they fade and lose their vibrancy. Her own parents' lives changed focus resultant to the impact of WWII and after. The 1950s became a pendulum swinging away from the raw sweat, blood, and tears of a nation at war to its opposite stance of superficial feel-good materialism.

Ferncliff Estate moved from a place where people gathered for salons on art, philosophy, features of the occult and a safe harbor for dying clairvoyants like Edgar Cayce to a benign gentleman's estate. Bernadette and Moncure were married and living in Charlottesville in the early 1940s when Mr. Cayce and his wife came to Ferncliff under her parents' invitation to spend his final days. At that time, Bernadette was helping Moncure build his practice while the war raged in Europe. She visited at Ferncliff one time and met Mr. and Mrs. Cayce, but it wasn't until after his death did she learn about the extent of his prolific career.

Bernadette made a visit to his center for research and enlightenment in Virginia Beach and was staggered by his most unusual life as a clairvoyant and healer. As these memories continued to come back to her on her drive through the Scottish highlands, Bernadette could feel something inside herself homing into this part of the world. *I used to live here.* This thought stepped forward in her brain as clear and vivid as if a voice spoke it out loud. She glanced around through the compact windshield and windows at the mountainous terrain of peat, heather, and cropped vegetation protruded by rocks. The landscape was wild and completely free of human encroachment. As her little rental car buzzed along the road, she was consumed by a clear sense of a past life once lived here, in an ancient castle by a lake. It was a warring time, with constant loss and casualty. And sorrow, such a great sorrow. As flecks of knowing another time unfolded in her head, she grasped at this possibility, a past life in Scotland, and she began to feel a deep sadness swell within her throat, clutching at her heart.

The car slowed down as if in response and acknowledgment, for now tears were welling up in her eyes. She brought the car to a halt on the narrow road and noted she was alone, not another vehicle in sight. Bernadette stepped out of the car to stretch her legs, breathe, and collect herself. She rubbed her arms; the cashmere sweater suddenly seemed flimsy against the Scottish winds. She guessed it was around one o'clock in the afternoon and roused herself to keep going, wanting to get to Rathven before dinner. Looking at the map, she revisited the routes and continued her drive.

A small handmade wooden sign on a post reading "Rathven Camp" with an arrow pointing left, one kilometer, came into view, and Bernadette made the turn. The sandy lane was bumpy and worn, her car was not as adept on this terrain, so she slowed to a cautious crawl. The lane was bordered by seagrasses and great wood rush, with a sprinkling of small purple flowers called primula. Though the day was still overcast, the sky seemed brighter, closer to the coast. After a painfully slow approach, the compound known as the Rathven community came into a view.

Quite unimpressive, Bernadette thought. The grounds were rustic at best, with a hub of RV trailers, or caravans as the British called them, randomly lined up to the right of a small cabin. A pair of old bicycles leaned against the cabin wall. Worn footpaths had developed from everyday traversing around the grounds and leading to heaps of sandy dirt—*I guess it's dirt,* Bernadette thought—with monstrous-sized plants sprawling from these mounds and flowers, everywhere flowers, rising from the sandy earth reaching for the sun, speckling the pale landscape with dots of color. A woman dressed in casual cotton garb, her head wrapped in a bandana and a garden basket slung over her arm, approached from one of the footpaths emerging from a sand dune.

"Hello! Welcome, pilgrim!"

She came up to the car, and Bernadette stepped out of the vehicle. Suddenly, her own clothing seemed too manicured and tailored for this place.

"Hello."

"I'm Jenny. You must be Bernadette. We've been expecting you. Come."

Jenny motioned for Bernadette to follow her into the cabin, which was the office of Rathven. It fit the appearance of the grounds, with heaps and mounds of papers, baskets, garden tools, surfaces covered with jugs, jars, aluminum flats of drying seeds and herbs.

"Excuse the mess." Jenny smiled, seeing Bernadette's gaze sweeping the room. "We just need you to sign in to the guest logbook, and I'll show you to the guest caravan." Jenny was English, her accent gently lilting and clipping words with emphasis on different syllables, and she was calm and sweet, Bernadette thought. "You've come from America? You must be tired. I will show you the dining house, and you can help yourself to coffee, tea, and snacks."

Bernadette was instructed to drive her car down the lane to the last caravan in the row and park it adjacent. There were scant few other cars. "How do people get here without cars?" Bernadette mused out loud.

Jenny laughed. "Many hitchhike out or get dropped off. Some bicycle from the villages nearby. I believe you are reserved for two weeks? Another woman will be arriving in three days and will be sharing your caravan. She is German. Her name is Frieda. Inside, you will find a printed schedule of daily activities, mealtimes, and orientation. As you know, this is a working retreat. Everyone helps with the work to share the load, and we have our meditations in the evenings. Sometimes Michael, Ellen, or Dottie will give special talks. Michael is away this week. You are familiar with our leaders?"

"Yes, I've been reading up on this community. Dottie is the one who telepathically communicates with angels. Michael and Ellen started the place, yes, thank you. I've been drawn to Scotland for many years. I, um, I need to clear my head."

"The sea air, the work, the love, the teachings, all of that will help you then," Jenny said softly. "And now the dining hall is right across the way." She pointed out the door. "We eat dinner, as you Americans call it, in about an hour." And she exited out the door, trotting away with her garden basket.

Bernadette lifted her suitcase on a twin bed and looked around to see if she could unpack. Otherwise, she would be living out of suitcase in this tiny space. The old Bailey caravan was well-worn but kept reasonably clean and tidy.

As she put away her things in drawers and shelves, she felt keenly strange and far from the familiar of home. Her departing flight from Washington, D.C. Dulles airport took place late in the day, and only her driver was aware of her plans. He scowled frequently on the way to the airport when he learned how impromptu her trip was, fretting about Mr. Robinson's well-being. (It was always the men we had to take care of as if they were some kind of fragile shell, as if she didn't feel guilty enough already). She thought about her parents and how they would have reacted to this trip she was making. Mother would have called it an adventure. Father would have been intrigued and researched everything ahead of time, drawing out scholarly and historical pieces of information to pepper the journey and make it all seem important and worthy. She decided to channel her parents' perspective, people way ahead of their time, she realized now. They had not been tied to the traditional life she married into.

Bernadette changed into sturdier clothing and shoes and stepped outside to explore this garden community. The wind whipped a humid but cool ocean air around her as she strolled down a path leading away from the main encampment and dining hall. The path scored through a grassy curve in the bay, and she could look back to the Rathven camp. The sun was still dominating the sky in the long hours of summer in the northern latitude, and low mountain ranges reclined further away. She walked along the scrub grass and sandy coast toward the other end of the camp, where the gardens were appearing in a riot of robust plants, flowers, and trees. She approached the coastal edge of the garden, and a man dressed in safari shirt and khaki britches stepped out from a row of sunflowers, startling her.

"Oh, excuse me," she said, and the man nodded. They stood briefly staring at each other without speaking. He appeared to be in his twenties or thirties; it was hard to tell. "Hello. I'm Bernadette, just arrived, trying to get the lay of the land. Beautiful plants you have here," she said, gesturing with her arm.

"They're not mine. I'm a visitor too," the man said. "I'm a reporter, come up from Newcastle. Got wind of this place growing plants in sandy soil and salt water. Doesn't seem possible, but here it is. Sunflowers in Northern Scotland? Unbelievable. But here they are!" He ran his hand down the stalk of one of the unlikely creations. Bernadette saw a flicker of movement behind him in the dense foliage of the sunflowers. She stepped to the side, and the reporter turned. "What?"

"Oh, it's nothing. Thought I saw a movement, didn't know if someone else was coming through."

The warm light in the sky blotted her mind, and Bernadette was overcome by a wave of jetlag. She excused herself to walk back to her caravan, and the reporter offered to accompany her. They strolled back through the arboretum of impossible plants, and Bernadette felt a crackle of electrical ions in the air generating from these plants. Something was weird here. The reporter postulated his editor's opinion that nuclear energy was involved. Bernadette turned sideways to look at him.

"Nuclear energy? Oh, come on."

The reporter shrugged with his hands. "So I'm here to find out." They parted on the path at the dining hall. "I'm Shamus, by the way.

There's a talk tonight at seven o'clock. In the hall. If you're not too tired."

"I'll have to take a raincheck. See you around."

Bernadette collapsed in her little bed to enjoy a few nights alone before a roommate arrived. Her head would have to sort things out tomorrow. She slept hard for twelve hours.

CHAPTER 8

THE FOLLOWING DAYS and nights at Rathven unfolded with characters and plot twists to rival a staged theatrical production. As Bernadette met other visitors and staff each day, she found the diversity both refreshing and amusing. Many of the visitors were earnest seekers of a spiritual awakening or communion with the divine. A certain ingratiating humility permeated their interactions, including small bows and greetings of "namaste" or "peace out," and a sense of harmony was perpetuated on the surface. Bernadette attended her first evening talk by one of the leaders named Dottie, who communed in first person with God and talked about the expansiveness of the universe and need for each person to explore their own inner depths. A guided meditation rounded out the evening, where attendees sat on cushions or chairs, and an initiate rang several singing bowls and chimes.

After a few days, Bernadette found herself gravitating to the company of the reporter, for he approached the whole scene with a ration of skepticism and science. Bernadette asked him about his research, and he seemed grateful to run his interviews and information by another witness.

"So they are all saying the same thing. The plants grow here because they have found the interface between humans and nature spirits, and they intentionally communicate, I guess through telepathy and intuition, with each other to determine where and when to be planted, and there's not much more than that. The spirit of nature does the rest. My editor won't sanction this story, I can tell you that much."

Bernadette smiled. "I'm not really adapting to this scene myself. I expected it to be more like a spiritual retreat, not a work camp."

By now, in their conversations, Shamus knew of her marriage, her home in Virginia, the life she found herself entrenched in, and this wild idea to run away to Scotland.

"Will you be leaving soon then?" Shamus asked.

"I've not decided yet."

The next day, after her roommate, Frieda, arrived, Bernadette discovered the woman wouldn't stop talking whenever they were together, so Bernadette made herself busy in the garden as much as possible. Early in the morning, she was kneeling inside a patch of pumpkins and gourds, when she felt eyes on her. She looked up from under her straw hat and saw a small elfish man crouched among the plants, gazing at her. Bernadette stared back at him, trying to comprehend exactly what she was seeing. He waved and gave her a crooked little smile.

"Who are you?" Bernadette called out. The man scootched a little further out of the plant stalks.

"I'm Sadis. Can you see me?" he asked with a look of fear and excitement at the same time.

"Yes. Am I supposed to?"

"One never knows with the humans. They are so oblivious sometimes about the existence of others, like me, from other realms. We're all around you humans quite a bit more than you realize. It's harder for us to materialize inside your buildings. So far, we seem to travel best between settings in nature. Here in Scotland, all the British Isles, actually, we have found millennia of recognition, not always good, among the human folk."

"What realm are you from?"

"We believe it is a fourth dimension. Parallel time but different place. My home is called Demistrath."

"Demistrath. I know that name. When I was a little girl in Virginia, I had playmates from there. How can you be here in Scotland too?"

"We travel between realms, mostly to help the humans with aspects of nature. Most humans have lost their connection to the cycles of nature. Michael here in Rathven, he broke through to our realm. In Demistrath, we are master gardeners, and he found us. We help him grow things. He is in sync with the laws of attraction, and we work collaboratively with him."

Bernadette felt oddly drawn to Sadis as he carried the same personal aspects of her childhood friends Astrid and Festus. How strange to be reminded of them yet again on this unruly adventure she was on.

"Do you know Astrid and Festus? Are they still in Demistrath?"

"Quite certainly, madame. Astrid is our village sage, and Festus is our chief carpenter. They are also on the council, and they know you have traveled here. Did you know, madame, you are called a Polaris in our world? Someone who functions as a hub for the convergence of energies, vibrations, ideas, and even beings?"

Bernadette stared at Sadis. "Polaris? I doubt that. I have suppressed my connection to other worlds for years now, Sadis. I don't know if we have anything like a Polaris in our world. My parents were very interested in the metaphysical aspects of spirituality when I was young. But I was never initiated into their gatherings. We have mediums and people who channel knowledge and messages from the other side. Maybe that is similar."

"A Polaris is a special thing, very important in holding the realms together. Without them, our two realms would never open up to each other like you and I are doing right now. You have many Polarises in your world, madame. Many just don't know how special their gifts are. Most are quite in tune as children, but they lose their connection as they get older. Humans as a whole have stopped believing in magic and metaphysical energy. Have you talked with Michael yet? He would be very interested in you and your gifts. He is a Polaris as well."

"I have not met him yet. Apparently, he is traveling somewhere this week."

"You must meet him. I believe that is one reason you were inspired to make this trip. I must depart now, madame."

"It was a pleasure meeting you." And before Bernadette could say more, he vanished from the earth.

Bernadette sat on the ground among rows of young pumpkins and gourds, wondering about what just happened.

She took a deep breath and decided she was not losing her mind but simply reawakening something familiar and lost. A rush of feeling for her parents consumed her, and she felt close to them, pulling on the threads of their memory to shed light on the stroke of magic she found herself swathed in again. She tried to remember her visits with Astrid and Festus more clearly, searching the folds in her brain. She must have been as young as five or six years, and it may have happened for several years as she remembered going to Warm Springs every summer for a while there. And now Sadis, another being from their realm, appeared to her and conversed so kindly.

"Is this supposed to mean anything? Am I supposed to do anything? Or is it just some sort of benign gap in the energy fields, and I get to glimpse between them? He called me a Polaris, which bodes a bit of distinction, but what am I to do with that?"

Bernadette stood in the gray damp morning, mist from the sea beginning to disperse, as the sun climbed above the horizon in a pale form of its blazing self. Instinctively, she raised her arms in an ancient sun salute, drawing the energy into herself.

Bernadette attended the evening gathering, where Dottie was giving a lecture on ego as friend or foe and how humans seem to have a plethora of ego, more so than many other beings in the celestial universes, so the spiritual question for the night was how to use one's ego-driven aspects for the betterment of the earth and others. Bernadette listened, wondering if Dottie's query was even possible since the very nature of one's ego was to be assertive, a leader, competitive, and dominant. *As a species, we seem pretty good at that,* she thought. *Survival of the species, stay alive at all costs, even if it means eliminating the other.*

The lecture was suddenly disturbed by a bevy of voices stirring in surprise and excitement at the back of the room, and as everyone was turning to see what was happening, Dottie's voice over the microphone announced the unexpected arrival of Rathven's spiritual leader and CEO, Michael himself.

Bernadette turned to see a strapping middle-aged man with tousled ginger hair entering the aisle as his devotees began to reach out and swarm him and shake hands, give hugs, and welcome him warmly. He played the part well, Bernadette thought, a blend of leading man, pastor/priest, and president, not to mention a touch of celebrity. One woman burst into tears as Michael stopped to greet her. He patiently placed his broad hand on top of her head, closing his eyes briefly, and then moved on. Dottie turned the mic over to him, but as he began speaking, it was clear he did not need it.

"Brothers and sisters, it is good to be home! Welcome one and all. My trip to London went as well as can be expected when talking to a bunch of scientists about gardening at sea level!" The room twittered in warmth and appreciation.

Michael, it turned out, performed with mastery all the team building aspects of community. As a public speaker, he was almost manic in his thoughts as they plundered through the minds of his listeners, all trying to keep up with his views and facts and goals and heroics, nodding, clapping, responding with affirmative grunts, groans, and hums. For Bernadette's part, she was having a hard time following his enthusiastic train of thought. She glanced at Shamus, who appeared stoic with his usual blunted expression, the poker face of a judge.

Then surprisingly, Michael ceremoniously turned the meeting back over to Dottie and seated himself off to the side, becoming very still with eyes closed as if entering deep meditation. When Dottie closed the meeting, the community resumed their mingle, breaking into the small pairs and clusters that crowds do, with hushed conversations and occasional bursts of laughter, as they funneled out of the great hall. Bernadette found Shamus outside, and he walked with her toward her caravan.

"I learned something about Michael's trip," Shamus said in a quiet voice. "I've been doing some digging. I found a talker in the community today."

Bernadette saw the light was on in her caravan, meaning Frieda was inside already. "Let's walk further," she said to Shamus, and they proceeded down the footpath toward the shoreline. The moon was in her waxing gibbous phase, a full moon would be along shortly in a few days, and there was enough light to see one's way.

"Turns out this whole operation is bankrupt, if you will, and the township is complaining about the community and the traffic of outsiders it brings in. Michael went looking for funding, backup, a patron, or sponsor. It's a hard sell, of course. The scientific community calls him an imposter, although they dispatched one of their own to visit here a month ago, and he found the place astonishing, to use his phrase, and he was hushed up immediately and forbidden to speak with the press or write up his visit in their journals. You'd think this was some kind of rogue operation and the mafia trying to squash it!"

Bernadette laughed out loud as she padded ahead of Shamus on the footpath, and the sound of her laughter startled her a bit as she realized she couldn't remember the last time she laughed. She ached to tell someone about her little visitor this morning in the pumpkin patch, but a strong instinct to refrain practically held her mouth closed. "Not now," a voice whispered in her head. "OK," she murmured to the voice.

"Did you say something?" Shamus spoke as they stood side by side on the beach, gazing at the moonlight glimmering on the water.

"I have a bad habit of talking to myself sometimes," Bernadette responded. "A middle-aged married woman falls into that habit easily."

Shamus politely did not reply. She had no idea why she said that to him, but she realized her true thoughts were starting to babble out from her after years of living in the deeper recesses of her psyche. Bernadette had studied psychology at Mary Baldwin College and loved it, even planning to go on for her masters and doctorate, but that was when the mysterious and alluring figure of Moncure Robinson entered her life, and she chose the old archetypical path of the complicit woman blithely walking into her own entrapment in societal norms. She was more ashamed of this than anything else. The women's movement was teaching her to question assumptions and speak up, speak out, about what mattered to women and to oneself. But sadly, she felt it was too late to change her own life choices. Ferncliff Estate was an entity to be reckoned with, employing many people and carrying on her family's legacy. Moncure was suave and a smart businessman, and her parents seemed pleased with her choice to marry him, maybe feeling their only child would be well cared for but not giving as much concern for her psychological well-being.

"The financial aspect then, of Rathven, is that a story for your paper?" Bernadette mused aloud, and Shamus turned suddenly to look at her.

"By Jove, ma'am, what an idea!" Shamus started to leave and then stopped. "Thank you for that idea. Is it all right if I go? You're OK here?"

Bernadette laughed again. "I am, Mr. Reporter! You go on now!" and she waved him away like a queen shooing away her minions. She stood awhile longer in the moonlight, listening to her heart, mind, and intuition. She no longer felt like a voyeur in someone else's world. She was a well-planted character in this particular play, holding forth on the stage, and she felt more alive than she had in a long, long time. Looking up at the moon, Bernadette said, "I must connect with Demistrath again, Mother." The moon spread her glow from her distant spot in the sky. Her love shone down in a silent veil of softness, but feeling the love was up to the skygazer.

CHAPTER 9

I T WAS HARD to sleep that night as the moon shone brightly into the porthole window of the little caravan where she slept. Her roommate was snoring lightly from the other side where the divan pulled out into a second bed. Bernadette finally gave in to the moon, pulled her shoes on, wrapped a small plaid blanket around her shoulders, and quietly stepped out into the night.

Without much thought, she walked to the garden side of the campus. All was quiet and peaceful, the moon bathing the landscape with the softest of silver light. A movement in a nearby lingonberry patch summonsed her attention, and two small figures were waiting for her. Even this did not surprise her. Everything now was taking place without her direction. It was an unfolding. Bernadette approached the two visitors. She recognized Sadis, while the other elven man started to beam at her.

"Ah, it is you, Ms. Bernadette, all grown up and shining so beautifully! We had no trouble finding you from our world."

It was Festus himself all grown up now too, wearing a leather tunic and stout boots, his muscled arms and gnarled hands indicative of an artisan laborer. He stepped forward and bowed deeply, and Bernadette knelt before him, extending her hands, which he took and squeezed in greeting.

"As you can see, we don't grow that much bigger, but you, my lady, you are dazzling!"

Bernadette laughed and seated herself on the ground, facing her two visitors. "No need for all that pomp, Festus! It is good to see you again. Little did I know I'd find you here in Scotland, on this crazy trip I made. Back home, I am definitely the talk of the estate, I'm sure. I've been remembering you and Astrid so often lately. The moon called me out tonight. Oh, how is she?"

"The moon is beneficent, as you can see, and Astrid sends her love," Festus chimed back, falling into the playful banter of their childhood. Bernadette and her two friends chatted amiably with laughs and warmth. Then Sadis cleared his throat and nudged Festus.

"Oh, quite right, duty calls." Festus changed his bearing to a more formal stance. He solemnly reached for her hand, and in it placed a small cluster of lingonberries. Bernadette looked at the small ripe berries and thought about the jellies her mother would make when she was a child. "Bernadette, we have a message and a mission for you. We are in need of your help. We need you to intervene with Michael. You see, we have become aware that his endeavor of gardening in these parts is no longer in balance with the source. It is taking a strain on our nature spirits, and it is impacting our home, Demistrath, to the point our own agriculture and farming is compromised. We have noticed a shift in our seasons and climate, and winters are harsher and longer. As you remember, we are an agrarian people, not hunters and warriors, so this is impacting us at many levels." He paused and searched Bernadette's face.

Bernadette was listening intently. She noticed the thoughts in her head were rapidly flashing through her awareness like pages in a book being fanned by a hand looking for a certain page and passage. Many of the thoughts were old repetitions of societal teachings and beliefs that infiltrate a person's consciousness, most of it was nonsense and negative, flavored with fear and ignorance. Thoughts like *Don't believe this*, *It's crazy talk*, *It's a trap*, *Don't bite*, *You're nuts*, *You're dreaming*, *You're gullible*, *You're stupid*. The moonlight surrounded her and fell on the faces of her two friends, imploring her for assistance. The page in her thoughts that she stopped on contained a simple direct message—remember, believe, and help. She looked up at the sky, and a silver aura or halo surrounded the speckled face of the moon. She felt a calm radiate through her mind and body.

"I will help you, but I will need more information. Michael returned to Rathven this evening, ahead of schedule. I will try to get an appointment with him. But is he aware of this problem? Would he even listen to me?"

"Tell him you are a Polaris too, that you have talked with us, and you know what's going on. Ask him to pull back and release the nature spirits from this garden project."

"But why can't the spirits excuse themselves and draw away from the project? Have they no free will in this matter?"

Sadis and Festus looked forlorn. "This, madame, is where we lack understanding. Our old ways tell us that when choices are made, the path unfolds in that direction to its fruition, and one is not able to 'jump off' the wagon, so to speak, once a choice is made. The spirits are without guile. They are innocent and perfect in their energies. But we believe this has made them vulnerable to dark magic."

Bernadette felt their sadness. She glimpsed the suffering of the Demistrathians for centuries, toiling for existence, believing they must remain in a single destiny chosen on a single day, often in innocence and naivete. *We are all the same,* she mused, *even those in the ethereal world, the spirit world, still susceptible to insufficient knowledge and limited by single belief systems.* She understood their reference to dark magic was the same as the human's framework of good and evil as the archetypical battle between God and Satan.

She shook her head. "The power of myths pervades us all. I'm sorry for the hardship you have all been through. You have my word, I will do everything in my power to help you." She was surprised at her own clarity here in Scotland. She felt so different from her Virginia self, stronger, freer, more in command of her own experience. She liked this feeling very much.

The two men simultaneously exhaled and relaxed. She wanted to just scoop them up in her arms for a group hug but restrained, wanting more to preserve their dignity and self-respect. Instead, they said their goodbyes, promising to meet up soon. Once again, they vanished into thin air, as the saying goes. Bernadette noticed this time a feeling of yearning as her other realmly friends departed.

The next day came sooner than she wanted as her night was shortened by her garden visit. Frieda was up and sitting with a cup of coffee, smoking a cigarette outside on the caravan's doorstep. Bernadette dressed and splashed her face with water from the tiny birdbath of a sink in the narrow sleeve of a toilet. Fireda heard her movements and began her chatter.

"Guten Tag, friend! Good morning! You slept late! The coffee is running low this morning. You must get some."

Bernadette stepped outside as Frieda stood to make way.

Frieda continued. "Michael is meeting with all the new guests in the garden this morning. He wants to welcome us all."

The sun was already warming the air, so Bernadette grabbed her hat and walked over to the dining hall to fetch some coffee and a roll. She walked with Frieda to the garden, allowing her roommate to hold sway with a variety of comments and observations. Bernadette listened with some distance, amassing her own thoughts about her mission with Michael. A small group of people were gathering by the sunflowers, among them Shamus, the reporter. He caught her eye in greeting with a nod. He appeared tired; she imagined he must have been writing last night. The other guests were greeting one another and brushing up on names and places of origin. At one point, Bernadette became aware everyone was looking at her with interest.

Frieda jumped in, saying, "This is Bernadette from Virginia," and Bernadette snapped into attention.

"Yes, sorry, still waking up. Yes, I'm American."

Michael rounded the bend of the flowerbeds, a clamor of energies preceding him, stirring the morning air with a buzz. He was dressed in overalls, work boots, and wearing the saddest, most beat-up straw hat still functioning on a human head. "Good, good morning, pilgrims! Welcome! Welcome!" His smile was infectious as he grasped and shook each person's hand, leaning in to repeat their name and arrival date to the community.

"I trust you have already learned much about this place and our harmonious work with nature. Come, I want you to taste our newest crop. We are expanding our research to find ways to grow nutritious crops in barren wastelands. Imagine a way to feed the hungry nations of this world!" With that, he led us over to the outer perimeter of the gardens and thrust his hands into mounds of sand and organic compost and revealed a bunch of carrots, small fingerling size in various colors.

"These, my friends, are our newest food addition to the Rathven gardens, another miracle, for the sustenance of humankind!" He found a nearby bucket with standing water and rinsed the bundle of carrots, separating them apart, one for each of us. Bernadette held the baby carrot and noticed the others, including Michael, munch on their carrots, nodding in approval. She took a bite; it was tasty. Shamus was also chewing without committing to a reaction, his face unmoved.

"Son, what are your thoughts?" Michael didn't miss a thing. Bernadette did not want to be drawn out, so she feigned interest in the smell and shape of the carrot, waiting for Shamus to respond.

"Impressive, I presume," Shamus said, "except that I have never liked carrots."

Michael burst into a roar of laughter, slapping Shamus on the back. Shamus looked mildly uncomfortable. Michael continued his focus on him, saying, "So tell me, what brings you here?"

Michael led him forward with a hand on his shoulder as the rest of the newcomers followed in a slightly delayed manner. All of Michael's moves were quick and without ceremony; he moved much faster and without pause or preparation than the average person. *Almost like a magician's sleight of hand,* Bernadette thought.

She would have to ask Shamus later how the rest of that conversation went as it was conducted out of earshot of the group. Michael stayed with the newest arrivals a few more minutes, enough for them all to feel important, and then dismissed everyone off to their morning "acts of service to the divine."

Bernadette suddenly realized she might not have such close access to Michael again and scurried up behind him as he sauntered away in the direction of the office.

"Excuse me, Mr. Haddy, may I have a word?"

Michael spun around and flashed a warm smile. "That may be all I have time for this morning. How can I help?"

Bernadette was suddenly searching for words and trying to discern how much to say in such rushed parameters. "This might be better discussed by appointment."

Michael arched an eyebrow, and then his face broke into another smile. "I left the corporate world a long time ago. We don't make appointments here at Rathven. Follow me, and we can talk as we go. As an American, what do you think of our endeavor here? I know the Americans are ahead of much of the world in agricultural advancements, experimenting with generous use of pesticides and fertilizers to boost production."

"I actually want to talk about the nature spirits, Mr. Haddy." Michael's face clouded over.

"You know about them, do you? I stopped sharing that information freely after it seemed to draw too many insincere people to our little plot of Eden here." He paused at the office entrance, wiping his hands on his overalls before opening the door. "Come in."

Bernadette was surprised how this conversation was happening so effortlessly. She followed him in. Jenny, the welcoming pilgrim, was working at a counter full of seedling plants in black plastic greenhouse flats, which were lit by low hanging fluorescent tube bulbs. She was misting them with water. Michael greeted her and asked her to check on the blackberries. She demurred with a soft "Namaste" and left the office. Bernadette marveled at his command; everyone seemed to fold, yield, step back, step aside, acquiesce to his pleasure.

"Nature spirits. Talk." He sat on the edge of the desk, his arms folded across his chest. His red hair sprawling around his face, his sad straw hat had been removed at the door. Bernadette was jolted by his sudden change in demeanor. He went on. "I will not defend or give testimony to nonbelievers. If you are here to challenge me, this conversation will be over."

Bernadette stared at him. "Quite the opposite, actually. I do believe in them. I know their kind. The small folk of Demistrath are my friends. It's a long story. I am a Polaris, same as you, Mr. Haddy."

"A what?" he roared back. "I don't know what you are saying. Look, madame, I am a simple man devoted to the almighty God. It is through his divine hand I am blessed with the help of the nature spirits. God is Lord of all. For some reason, HE has given me guidance on growing this garden."

Bernadette decided to plunge on, not sure now where this was going to go. "While working here, have you never met a small elven person?"

"The wee folk? Are you serious? I am a Brit. I suppose I must believe, huh? I have had to put those thoughts and memories from my childhood behind me, madame, for I am no longer a child. I am a man who abides with the Lord God, and I don't see the wee folk anymore. He does not show them to me. They are of the past."

"OK, so let's talk about the nature spirits then. I have been visited by their messengers who have informed me the nature spirits are overwhelmed keeping up with the monumental scale of this garden and the demands put upon them to perform. They are growing sick and tired. They can't keep this up at this pace. They have beseeched me to speak with you."

Michael stood, thrusting his hands into his overalls. Bernadette could see he was struggling to control several emotions: anger, fear, forcing patience. "I can't accept what you are saying. I believe the Lord God is all powerful and all knowing and would not, nay, cannot run out of life giving energy. Wherever you got your information, it is not correct. The ONLY reason this place exists is because WE believe in eternal love, without limit, and that GOD is blessing us to serve as examples of what is possible if we simply believe and obey."

He locked eyes with Bernadette, and they stood in silence facing each other. "Do I have your word that this conversation will remain confidential? Not just for the sake of our endeavor here but for yours as well. The community will exorcise you if you speak like this. It will not be tolerated."

CHAPTER 10

"**I** WAS BASICALLY SHUNNED by Michael after that," Bernadette said to me in the wooded encampment by the stream. "I remained a few more days. I had one more visit from Sadis and Festus, and they were keenly disappointed. Shamus left for Newcastle and told me to keep in touch. As you have probably deduced by now, I did keep in touch with him. When I left Rathven, I traveled to Edinburgh then down into England. I stayed in Britain for five weeks. I had sent another letter to Moncure, and we had one long-distance telephone call, where he basically demanded I cease this nonsense and return home. Shamus met me in Newcastle, and we talked quite a bit about what happened in Rathven. His story about Rathven got published but faded from public thought after that. I felt so sorry and ashamed I couldn't help my friends in Demistrath, and the whole runaway wife adventure turned sour sadly. I returned home with my tail between my legs, and Moncure gave me the silent treatment for a week."

Ms. Bernadette's story weighed heavy in the air as I listened while the ill-fated adventure started to unravel. I reached out a hand to hers and squeezed it. "You did a brave thing for your time, Ms. Bernadette."

"So out of character for me. I felt humiliated. I stashed all my experiences deep into my memory and hid them away. I patiently waited for Moncure to talk to me again, which he did, and not surprisingly, he never mentioned my episode again. I started painting canvases of my faint memories of Demistrath that became more vivid over the ensuing months - of rolling hills and fairy folk - but also of Rathven and dark scenes of nature spirits being choked by burly men like Michael. The Ferncliff staff became troubled by my demeanor. I must say, Eva, they thought I had gone completely mad, but I cannot blame them."

Bernadette stopped and caressed her hands together in her lap. She glanced over at me, and I gave her my best encouraging smile. "One of my saddest memories is the face of Sadis when I let him know my talk with Michael backfired. Festus tried to be encouraging, I guess because he was my friend first, but Sadis's face, Eva, I will never forget." She paused and looked away, and I could tell by her face she had grown tired.

"Why don't you rest a spell? Can I get anything for you?"

She was quiet for a while, and I busied myself with looking through the luncheon basket, pulling out a thermos of hot tea and milk. I poured some in a copper mug and handed it to Ms. B. She held the mug but did not drink.

We made another trip to Demistrath that morning. I think Ms. B. knew that would happen, but I sure didn't. Mr. Dabbs appeared in the circle of stones and approached us at the stream. He looked apprehensive, but kindness remained in his eyes. I realized this morning he was a very special person with above-average fairy powers. I was quite certain his ability to move the two of us through dimension and space was not imbued into every Demistrathian.

"It is good to see the two of you this morning. I am glad that last night did not keep you away. I have gathered the inner council together in Lara's home, and they await your attendance." He looked between Ms. B. and myself. "If you would be so kind."

Ms. B. placed her mug on the folding table and rose to stand. I joined her at her side. "We can leave everything just so. It will appear we went on a walk should anyone pass by."

The three of us joined hands in the stone circle and disappeared from Warm Springs, Virginia.

Demistrath sparkled in a dewy summer morning, with glistening grassy slopes and sunlight dancing on the flowers and trees. We took the now familiar hillside footpath down to Lara's cottage. I could see so much more detail in today's light. The morning fish market was already in place, with various vendors and workers peacefully moving around tethered boats, navigating around heaps of fishnets and buoys being sorted for the day's fishing expeditions. A few folk were passing both ways over the bridge, carrying baskets, pushing wheel barrels, or guiding a goat, cow, or donkey to their next chapter of life. I wanted to stay and watch this quaint and alluring Hobbit-like scene all day, but we reached the cottage.

Inside, once again gathered around Lara's table, I recognized Festus and Astrid, Lara, the heretofore unnamed Bavarian, and two other new faces. We were greeted with a mixture of relief, expectation, and guarded acceptance. Ms. B. was steered toward one of the chairs. Pots of tea and plates of scones and tarts covered the table.

Astrid sounded a small brass chime with a felted mallet, and the room grew quiet. "Brothers and sisters, we call this meeting to light and clarity. This meeting is kept sacred and remains private until further unfolding." She then began stating each person's name, and they answered the roll call.

Festus said, "Aye."

Lara answered, "With open hearth."

Bernadette stated, "Here."

Gunter (the Bavarian) declared, "Ya."

Dabbs uttered, "At your service."

Egeria (new face) responded, "Yes."

Lurien (new face) commented, "I am here."

Eva. Silence.

I was so riveted to Lurien. I didn't know why I was hearing my name. I felt a nudge to my ribs from someone's elbow. Lamely, I heard myself echo the words I just heard. "I am here."

Lurien was standing away from the table with one foot propped on a stool, a pair of strong hands gently whittling a piece of wood with a knife. This person raised their eyes and met mine, a small smile curved on one side of their mouth, and then the hands resumed the whittling. I could feel my face flushing as I forced myself to look back around the table. Astrid was watching me closely.

"Egeria is our water witch," Astrid began, introducing the newcomers to Ms. B. and me. "Gunter is our metalsmith. Lara is the keeper of the hearth and fire. Dabbs is the lord of the air. Festus is the master of the woods. And Lurien is our protector."

Bernadette looked around the circle. "The Council of the Elements. I am honored." She gave a little bow.

I was standing behind her and felt oddly out of place. I had no title, no history with these people, and I was quite sure they were probably tolerating me. I was also still embarrassed by my reaction to Lurien. Mind you, I was not a giddy girly crush-type person. In fact, I was much happier not bothering with those irksome emotions. I learned to keep my intimate thoughts and feelings deeply embedded in my own heart and mind and never shared with others. I rarely was attracted to someone, and if I was, I would always reject it as frivolous and superficial. I didn't have time for the moonstruck antics of the romantic. I could see the damage it did by watching others. No, not for me. Too many other important ways to use my emotions and my brain.

As the meeting unfolded, I would steal glances at Lurien. I couldn't tell if I was looking at a man or a woman. This person was well-built and muscled yet slim in the torso and the faintest curve of breasts. The hair was cut in an asymmetrical way, with a curtain of straight chestnut bangs sweeping to one side and the other side cut out around the ear. A long tail braided from the back hung to one side, tied at the end with a leather cord from which a cluster of objects dangled like charms: a shell, a crystal, a copper coin. Lurien was wearing a hunter green leather hide jacket, with black leather leggings tucked into over-the-knee boots of a supple deep indigo blue leather. I also noticed a stout bow and quiver of arrows propped against the wall behind Lurien.

The Council of the Elements was deep in discussion about Dev Sinnot. There was question about his right to rule the Queendom as Demistrath had always been matriarchal in its royal dynasty. When a queen did not have a daughter, the closest female blood relative was next in line. When the last queen passed away suddenly, without a daughter, the Queendom was bereft and confused because the queen did not have a female next of kin. Dev Sinnott stepped in quietly and without fanfare, and the council assumed he would be temporary, but as his successor still remained unnamed days later, he grew more assertive in taking the role with presumption. Unbeknownst to the council, he brought in advisors to surround him with great interest and dedication. Some were from Demistrath, childhood friends most likely, but a couple others were new to the realm. I was gathering and assembling all this information rapidly from the meeting. Ms. Bernadette was equally transfixed, taking it all in with more alertness than I normally saw in her. Was it my imagination, or did Ms. B. seem more robust while in the realm of Demistrath?

"Astrid, you would be the queen's successor in your role as sage." Egeria was speaking now, peering up from a large old leatherbound book sprawled open on the table in front of her. "It says here in the event of non-bloodline lineage, the sage takes the queen's mantle."

"I was aware of that, my friends. But I have neither the heart nor the head for it. I serve best as a teacher and counselor."

"We must select someone from our council," Festus interjected. "Our queen would have wanted one of us to succeed her."

Ms. B. started to speak. "Why do you think she never named someone? That seems odd to me."

"We have known several generations of peacetime, my lady. The Demistrathians have grown softer in their approach to the Great Mother, the earth, and we consider ourselves artisans and gardeners. We trade and barter with the surrounding kingdoms to satisfy our simple earth-based lifestyle. A new generation of nature spirits has been quietly building their strength since the Rathven days, and we are producing more garden and game bounty and abundance. We love our rituals and celebrations, our exhibitions and festivals, our wine and ale, sweet cakes, and hard work. Our families are strong and fertile, and we have very little to fear at this time. I'm afraid to say it . . ." Mr. Dabbs paused. "But we have grown soft, and Sinnott is no fool. He's a wolf who came in while the sheep were grazing."

Lurien stirred in the corner and laid the carving on the stool. Even the voice I heard was androgynous, a sonorous tenor with an even tone and cadence. "The fact of the matter is the goddess has been forgotten in all this pastoral contentment, for she is the giver and taker of life, the sustainer and the destroyer, the source of the seasons. I have sworn the oath of protector of Demistrath, and I am here to serve, but I have not been given support for taking action in this matter. Say the word and I will arrest that upstart son of a queen."

I was still staring at Lurien, who stood with military bearing of readiness and attention, eyes flashing. My mind was racing between "he" and "she" as words to describe the charismatic Lurien wrestled in my head. Lurien's face was a perfect study of symmetry and balance, both handsome and beautiful. I was mortified to realize my heart was beating rapidly, and my breath was quick and shallow. The council began to mutter in side talk back and forth. Lurien remained silent and still, like a cat eyeing its target with intensity and nonchalance.

Astrid stood at her place at the table and let out a "ssshhh" to the room. "Silence!"

We heard Gunter mutter, "What does the gender bender know?"

Astrid sat back, folding her hands in front of her mouth. Lara looked bewildered, Festus began to twiddle his thumbs, Egeria quietly closed the book, and Mr. Dabbs walked to the head of the table beside Astrid and cleared his throat.

"If I may suggest, let us remember our visitors. We have brought them here for a purpose."

Lurien's eyes suddenly swept over to me and Bernadette, and I quickly looked down.

"As you can tell," Mr. Dabbs went on, "we are in disarray here as a council and lack an organized vision for our people. The queen's death has revealed our true status. We are not leaders, we are a democracy, and this unexpected usurper has placed us in a weak spot."

The council grew quiet and attentive as Mr. Dabbs continued. "I would like to redirect us back to our initial plan. Astrid and Festus suggested that we invite Lady Bernadette as a foil to forestall Sinnot's decree to modernize Demistrath. Our people are a blended tribe of gardeners, fishers, hunters, and artisans. We are both fairy folk and woodland folk, tall in statue or small, and we have coexisted quite well in a matriarchy." He turned to Lurien. "You mention the goddess. We have not forgotten her. She is still the blood in our veins and the source of our lives, but yes, we have allowed her dominion to fade more to the background, and rather than cowering to her cycles and whims, we have elected to consort with the more benign and softer arts of magic and curiosity, crafts and rituals."

Ms. B. spoke next. "Why don't you let your protector do as spoken and take back the queen's mantle? You have an army or sorts, I presume. As the Elemental Council, you all can sanction the action to the people." Before the council could respond, Ms. B. continued. She smiled at Lurien and said, "With respect, how are you known, my friend, as he or she?"

"I am neither and both. I am best referred to as they. There is no word for my kind yet."

Ms. B. nodded. "In this realm, maybe not." She then addressed the room. "As the Elemental Council, you share a complete array of skills and power designed to function in times of crisis and trouble. It was an early construct from many centuries ago, based on principles of science, physical matter, and alchemy, whereby the sum is as strong as its parts working together. Harmony and unity are essential for the Elemental Council to perform its tasks. Passivity is not. Perhaps it is time to bring back the true council, not the one that gathered last night at Dev Sinnot's Luhgnasa circle."

Ms. B. was tuned in and focused in a way I had rarely seen before. How she knew all this stuff, I was not sure. The council members were also paying her mind. Once again, small dyads of conversations began to issue from the table as the group began to brainstorm on the idea just generated. Lurien stirred and, to my chagrin, turned and grabbed the bow and arrows, bowed to the council, and started to leave the cottage.

"You can find me in the glade at the encampment, readying the guard troop."

Our eyes locked briefly, and then this person was gone, a draft of dancing energy swirling out of the room in the departure.

I don't remember much of what transpired after that, I'm afraid. I was too busy trying to subdue my body from the elevated vibration knocking through my bones, all the while reprimanding myself for losing my cool and composure in the presence of Lurien and the council.

Somehow it was decided to proceed with the plan posed by Ms. B., but I could tell the council was disturbed at the aggressive turn the situation was demanding of them. I did feel sorry for their turmoil, for the bucolic life of Demistrath was truly appealing, and I could deeply feel their chagrin at the direction this was taking. Denial is always easier, but it can erode any gains made, I suppose. Still, I felt sad for them.

Soon, there was a buzz between Ms. B. and Mr. Dabbs about transporting us back to Warm Springs. This bi-realm adventure was starting to become tedious. I wanted to stay here; this side of the world was much more interesting than my life in Virginia. I believe Ms. B. was feeling the same way. Without speaking, we shared the same thoughts—we must construct a way to be gone for a much longer length of time.

This back and forth every day was not going to be sustainable. And Demistrath needed us now, with the impending coup d'état or, more accurately, the push back on the invader. I sure hoped it would not become a battle or a war.

CHAPTER 11

T HE HUM OF the cicadas was the only sound back at our wooded stream. Everything was as we left it. I felt extremely discontent and somewhat disconnected from this reality. I busied myself setting out our lunch, my head spinning around what just transpired.

"I don't have much of an appetite, child, but Lord knows I'll force myself to eat as I can't insult the kind efforts of Shamus and Hans to provide for us."

"Ms. Bernadette, since Shamus knows of this other realm, and your encounters with the Demistrathians, couldn't we let him in on what we are doing? Would that help?"

"Shamus doesn't really know. There were several times I wanted to tell him, and something inside me forbade it. Even though I trust him, and he has been a friend all these years, I don't know him. He is a private person, as you can tell."

She went on, "We must find a way to stay in Demistrath longer. When we get home, I will arrange a retreat I must go on, and you too, of course, so Mr. Robinson and the staff won't worry."

I pondered what was starting to weigh in my mind, from the past number of days, all the old memories with Ms. B. coming up, the silent communications, her demeanor change in Demistrath. How were we connected, I wondered? Like I said, this was all new territory for me, the metaphysical, I guess you call it. Time travel, telepathy, past lives, clairvoyance, magic—words we humans put on these things we don't understand and can't prove or explain.

We nibbled at our lunch, and I couldn't help noticing it was really tasty. Shamus sure knew how to put together an interesting yet simple meal—a curried chicken salad, radishes and cucumber slices, crusty rolls, and sliced honey dew melon.

I daydreamed about Lurien, while Ms. B. grew quiet in her chair and then dozed off. I sat in silence with my thoughts, enjoying a little reprieve from all the action. The image of Lurien stood in my mind with vivid detail. But even more evident was the sensation of Lurien, the feel of their presence, the warm and vibrant energy of this person, so alive, so rich in soul, mind, and body. I was now longing for Lurien, wanting to see them again. Eventually, I found myself nodding off and into a deep, trancelike sleep.

I was flying, for lack of better word, into another place. It was like a vision, but I was in it except I was not seen because the people in this place clearly did not see me. The sun was shining in bright blue skies, and it was warm. Palm trees and oaks and various shrubs resembling subtropical vegetation surrounded me. I was moving along a brick street that lined a small canal of running water. Huge trees many stories high draped their foliage to create a canopy of shade. I noticed a couple walking arm in arm from the opposite direction on the other side of canal. The woman laughed. She was wearing a broad brimmed straw hat banded with a poofy arrangement of ribbon, lace, and feathers. She was dressed in a layered dress belted at the waist, circa 1900ish. The man was wearing a linen blazer and slacks and a boater hat and was telling her some kind of story that seemed to amuse her. As they drew closer, I could hear they were speaking in French.

They turned away from the canal and ascended a series of stone steps leading up to a large two-story, Victorian-style house with steeped attic and rimmed with gingerbread-carved cornices and valances. I followed them, still floating in the air like a spirit and found myself in the dark wood-lined foyer of the house. The couple were removing their hats and still chatting in French, which I didn't understand. She went into a sitting room, and he ventured out a back door to a covered porch and proceeded to smoke a small dark brown cigar. They appeared to be in their thirties, best I could tell. She was fanning herself with a simple fan and pulled open a small little book, starting to read it. Then she called out to him, "Jean Paul," several times, but he did not hear her.

The scene shifted, and the couple was now seated at a round dining room table. They were joined by others, and the room was dark, lit by a couple of lamps and some candles. In the center of the table was a deep glazed pottery bowl filled with dark water. As I peered even further, there were objects on the table—decks of colorful cards, little trinkets shaped like animals, totem-like figurines of a breasted female with swollen belly, arms circled above her head. A brass goblet stood beside a small plate with dried herbal leaves smoldering, letting off a musky scent in a curling wisp of smoke. The party of people were all holding hands on the table in silence with eyes closed.

I didn't think they were praying Christian prayers. This must be a séance. My curiosity was intent on learning what this entailed. I was then aware they were speaking in English. Lucky me. The French couple was bilingual.

"Welcome to Roser Park," an older gentleman was saying. "We gather as a salon on this night of the Lunar eclipse and midsummer celebration. We welcome our guests, Mr. and Mrs. Autry from Virginia. They have traveled to Florida at our invitation to share their knowledge of the occult, which has been passed for generations from their old ancestral lineage in France."

The table of guests smiled and nodded at the French couple and released their hands, settling into their chairs. The French couple must be Ms. Bernadette's parents, I realized! My mind rapidly calculated this scene must have happened before she was born. Before 1915, I guessed. I felt I was watching a hologram.

I felt a tingling sensation in my body, my heart beating with some excitement and fear, realizing I was witnessing something from that past. What unfolded around the table was a demonstration by the

Autrys of some ancient rituals used in Europe for calling on the gods and goddesses to inform, heal, predict, divine, and reveal spiritual aspects of life on Earth.

The bowl, or cauldron, was used to create tinctures of herbs and plants blended with fluids like tears, sweat, and blood to meld the bond between Earth and its human inhabitants.

"The bowl is used for creating something, whether a potion or an idea. It contains your desires and amplifies them." Mrs. Autry was saying.

"Fire, on the other hand," Mr. Autry softly added, "is used for destruction to rid yourself of that which you no longer need or want. Often, it is written on paper and ceremoniously burned.

"This process of 'like attracts like' is referred to as magic, the alchemy between word and deed, or thought and form, or desire and manifestation. Likened to divine creation, the rituals help bid into existence that which was not, and represent what life is all about on this planet. What you sow, so shall you reap."

The Autrys took turns speaking or teaching and helped connect the various religious and esoteric languages used to describe this process or experience, pointing out how each paradigm is describing something similar but in unique languages. They pointed out phrases and scriptures from the current major world religions and described how these beliefs were predated in time by pre Christian (BC) eras of Earth-based and indigenous spiritual practices and religious ceremonies.

I realized I was holding my breath to listen hard, not wanting to miss any of this dynamic information. I had never heard stuff like this before, but I was educated enough to recognize the terms and concepts, so to have knowledge imparted to fill in the blanks was captivating. I felt excited, I felt inspired, I felt less empty. I wanted to join this salon and broaden my knowledge and understanding. I puzzled how these types of teachings had become taboo, squashed, and disreputable by mainstream society and our political, academic, and religious institutions. In fact, this subject matter was deemed false, not real, wishful, untrue, nonsense. Yet was it?

"Eva! Eva! Wake up!" Someone was shaking my shoulder.

I felt myself sucked out of the Roser Park house, the salon room faded away, and I was opening my eyes to see Ms. B. and Hans standing over me with looks of concern on their faces.

"Are you all right, my dear? We couldn't wake you. Your eyes were fluttering, and your face was twitching. We were afraid you were having a stroke or a seizure. Talk to me. Are you OK?"

I pushed through my mental haze, catching my bearings. "The woods. At Warm Springs. The year is 1985. I'm Eva Mason, twenty years old. I work for you, Ms. Bernadette. Hans is our driver."

The two of them started to laugh in relief, and I realized I was speaking out loud. "Go on," Hans was saying. "What else? Where were you?"

"I was dreaming I was flying. I visited a place in Florida called Roser Park! How odd is that?"

"Ah, flying dreams, they are the best," Hans said with appreciation. He was starting to clean up our little luncheon campsite. Ms. B. continued to eye me with a quizzical look.

"Did you say Roser Park?"

"Yes, it was in Florida. A very vivid dream. I can remember every detail."

Ms. B. spoke quickly. "You can tell me later. We have to go back to the inn. Mr. Hans said a rainstorm is coming in. Shamus had to take a call from Ferncliff. Mr. Robinson apparently has fallen ill. We will have to cut this trip short and go home." She gave me one of her pointed stares, which I knew meant "Keep quiet. Follow orders. Don't ask questions. We will talk later."

I nodded and helped Hans gather our things, handing my boss her walking cane. *Back to Earth, silly girl,* I said to myself. No more Lurien. No more Mr. and Mrs. Autry. No more dimension travel. Back to business. I wondered what had happened to Mr. Robinson.

Ferncliff Estate was much as we had left it yesterday morning, although it felt like I had been away for a week, with all the adventures in Demistrath and all I had learned about Ms. B. and her runaway trip to Scotland. I had met so many people, it seemed, who were embroiled in important life-changing issues, and even though I apparently dreamed it, my visit to Roser Park and seeing the Autrys felt vividly real to me, like I had actually been there. On the ride home, I asked Ms. B. what her parents' names were, and she confirmed they were Jean Paul and Marie Autry. Bam. Since the men were in the car too, we couldn't talk about my vision or what to do about Demistrath. I tried to access the newly discovered telecommunication shared between us but could not break through to Ms. B., who sat staring out the window and was closed off to me.

Shamus had received the phone call from Ferncliff about Mr. Robinson falling ill and dispatched Hans to the woods to collect us. Thank God we had already returned from Demistrath, or Mr. Hans would have been desperately trying to locate us as lost. Apparently, Mr. Robinson was suffering from an alarming fever and strange aches and pains throughout his body. He was already taken to the hospital, and Ms. B. was back in the house with staff, who were filling her in on his affliction.

Ms. B. wanted to go to the hospital, of course, so Hans was gearing up the car for its next trip down the mountain. It was late afternoon, and I knew Ms. B. was probably worn out for the day. I wondered if she would ask me to go along. I was secretly hoping not; I was ready for some time alone with my thoughts. Shamus offered to accompany her, and she accepted.

The household would survive just fine without their head chef, especially since the household family was not at home. Staff had our own dining room off the kitchen and access to our own refrigerator of foods. The picnic hamper from Warm Springs was being unpacked and put away when I wandered into the kitchen. Betsy breezed in and pulled up a chair at the kitchen table.

"Whew, I'm tired. We did some deep cleaning while the missus was away. How was your vacation?" She was grinning at me, knowing I preferred not to be judged for some of the coveted assignments I was sent on as right-hand assistant to the queen bee. That was the moniker Betsy and I shared between us for our mistress. It was a term of affection, but the older staff would probably have objected to the usage.

"Well, I will say it was an adventure." I sat at the table with Betsy, pushing glasses of lemonade in front of each of us. "Bathing in the Warm Springs was quite nice. Very relaxing. We stayed in an old mill that had been converted to an inn. Very quaint."

Betsy looked around to make sure no one else was in the vicinity. "Did you find out anything more about that huge red stain on the carpet? We couldn't get it out. We had to roll up the carpet and send it off to the professional cleaners."

"Ms. B. said the stain came from berries, the lingonberry to be exact. But she never told me who put the stain on the carpet or why. It was not her."

"That sounds rather cryptic. No other clues?"

"Not that I can share," I said and looked away. I had better change the subject fast. Betsy was bright and curious and would keep pushing me. I knew my threshold for keeping secrets from my best friend was getting harder and harder. "I missed *Growing Pains* last night. Did you see it? What happened?"

"Not so fast, sister. What do you mean by the phrase 'that you can share'?"

"Betsy, you know I have to honor privacy in certain matters."

"But I'm not just anybody, Eva. I won't gossip. You know I won't."

I decided I could probably safely share some of the information about Ms. B.'s Scotland trip and meeting Shamus. That would probably satisfy Betsy, and it was the believable part of my adventure. I left out the part about Ms. B.'s encounters with Sadis and Festus by the lingonberry patch. As for telling her about the other realm? That I would have to keep a lid on.

"Let's go outside. I don't want Mrs. Rutledge charging in here midstream!"

I was not sure if I felt better after telling Betsy about Ms. B.'s Scotland trip. She was very curious about the Rathven community and the fantastical gardens. I was relieved that all I could say was only what I heard. If I had tried to tell her about Demistrath and inter-dimensional travel, I would be speaking from firsthand experience and most likely disbelieved, even labeled as crazy.

Back in my room at the estate, I popped an Elton John cassette in my little player and curled up on my bed with my journal and decided to write a little about my experiences. My dictionary was getting a lot more usage lately as I looked up words particularly related to metaphysics, realizing I had so much more to learn about this world. There was no one to talk to here at the estate who would remotely understand or not condemn me. I felt like an imposter, a voyeur floating around the perimeter of these mysteries, not really part of them but still given glimpses and snippets into these saturated lives of people both in my realm and in other realms, who lived this stuff wholeheartedly in contexts where it was the norm—Rathven, Demistrath, the salon group at Roser Park.

I then remembered the crystal Mr. Dabbs had given me to call for him, which I had stashed in my jeans pocket. I quickly jumped out of my bed and rummaged through my weekend bag and found it. Feeling relieved, I curled my hand around it and returned to my bed. This little stone felt precious to me now, a link to this other world, this whole other reality. I pondered my life in Virginia, at Ferncliff. When I thought of my family, I knew it no longer felt like my home. The cautionary tale of travel is beware. Your sense of belonging changes. I was on my own, and my years at Ferncliff had opened up a much larger world to me, from the one I started out in. Even at twenty, I knew I couldn't go back, nor did I want to.

CHAPTER 12

DURING THE NIGHT, I dreamed about a castle by the sea in Scotland. I was roaming from room to room, up and down circular stone steps, walking up to heavy dark wooden doors with iron fixtures, an enormous iron key in my hand. The key would fit into the keyhole but would not open the doors, which remained locked to me.

Betsy was shaking me awake. "Eva, get up. You've overslept! The mistress is up already. She's asking for you."

I sat upright, staring at Betsy. "Oh no. I'll be right there."

I dressed quickly in my uniform and tied a bandana over my braids after bundling them together with a hair tie. I splashed water on my face, staring at my reflection in the mirror. My eyes stared back at me. Eva. Eve. First woman. I shook my head, dried my face, hung up the towel, and strode out the room up the steps to the kitchen, where I passed Shamus at the stove.

"Good morning, Shamus."

"Aye, good mornin' to you, lass. Here, you can take her tray. It's ready."

I lifted the tray, laden with another breakfast, and asked about Mr. Robinson.

"He's still in ICU. But stable. Pneumonia maybe? Double pneumonia, I believe. Somethin' like that. Run along. Don't want the eggs to get cold."

I headed for Ms. Bernadette's room, realizing I now knew much more about Shamus than I did two days ago. He seemed friendlier to me since our Warm Springs trip.

I found Ms. B. sitting up in her bed, with a newspaper and other mail opened and unopened strewn around her.

"Oh, there you are, Eva."

"Sorry, I'm late, ma'am." I set the breakfast tray down and helped her arrange herself to take it in bed. I was glad to fall so easily back into our Ferncliff routine despite all the other thoughts and questions about what to do next that were prowling around in my head. I would need to follow Ms. B.'s lead with this Demistrath stuff.

As if to read my mind, once again, Ms. B. finished chewing her first bite and said, "Eva, you may have to return to Demistrath without me. I really need to stay here with Moncure. I shall have to send you as my emissary."

"But, ma'am, I can hardly replace you. My goodness, what a thought. I know nothing about political power plays and harnessing technology for agriculture and governmental overthrows!"

Ms. B. laughed. "And do you think I do, child? There has long been a connection between the realm where Demistrath lies and this one, where we live." Suddenly, she pushed her breakfast tray away and wiped her hands delicately on the linen napkin. She squared her gaze on me. "There is more you need to know, and I will tell you. It will help you understand the importance that one of us be represented with the Elemental Council in Demistrath."

She insisted on dressing and walking to the garden and the woods again today. I could see the importance of keeping these conversations private from passing ears and interruptions of the household. Mr. Hans was driving her back to the hospital at 1:00 p.m. On our walk, she explained I could ride into town with her, using some vacation time for a few days, and then make a longer stay in Demistrath. The issue to work out would be connecting with Mr. Dabbs for inter-realm transport. It would be so easy if I could just leave from the woods here, where we first encountered Mr. Dabbs. But how would my disappearance be explained to the staff?

This reminded me of a nagging question I wanted to ask her, about how I was identified as being a "beacon" at our first meeting with Mr. Dabbs. And more disturbing to me now was remembering how he said that Dev Sinnott detected my beacon. Ms. B. looked askance at the question; she too had not thought about that further.

"Mr. Dabbs will have to answer that question, Eva. What I need to tell you will probably sound even more unbelievable. I don't want to overwhelm you with so much so fast, but it is out of my hands." Bernadette paused by the lingonberry plants. My mind went back to that morning and remembered my déjà vu experience, where I could see the two of us looking into a dark bowl of water somewhere in medieval times.

When I become riveted by my own thoughts, I tend to speak out loud. So I said, "Have we shared another lifetime together?"

Ms. B. was startled, but then she let out a chuckle. "You may be picking up to this faster than I anticipated. Yes, we have. Does that idea seem believable to you? Many people see it as nonsense. For many, to believe in reincarnation would shatter their entire belief systems. But it was, and is, a commonplace belief all over this planet to this day. It's just not compatible with Christianity, and the belief was squashed by the Christian founders in the early centuries. I remember my parents explaining it to me, and I've always loved the idea. It confirms so many deep connections, don't you think, and so many mysterious features of life we sometimes call destiny?"

My mind was entranced by this new idea, and I could feel all my cogs and wheels spinning quickly through the paradigm and connecting the threads of meaning and implication embodied in the concept of reincarnation. "What part of us reincarnates? Our personality? Our spirit? Our soul?"

"I suppose the soul aspect of ourselves would best capture the idea of what reincarnates from lifetime to lifetime." Ms. B. plucked off a cluster of red juicy lingonberries and held them in the palm of her hand. "And the general assumption is that the soul, in between lifetimes, convenes with its spirit guides to decide the next best life opportunity to continue to work out one's purpose, although I think that's where things get murky and mysterious and unclear. The 'why' questions can never be answered clearly."

"So what lifetime do you think we have shared?" I asked. I hoped it would resemble my déjà vu memory because I wanted to know I could trust my own intuition. I wanted to think there was something purposeful happening to me right now and not just a jumble of strange dreams, insights, and psychic skills that I would find out later were signs I was going crazy. My heart was begging Ms. B. to organize the last three days for me. She smiled and handed the berries to me. I took them in the palm of my hand.

"Take a breath and calm your mind. Open your six senses and allow yourself to just experience the berries in your hand right now. Most of the time, we never notice our deep connection to all things. You have to train yourself to notice."

I did as she suggested. I was curious, and I sensed no danger in the request. It seemed natural and pleasant. I could feel the light sensation that I was holding something in my hand, the berries seemed weightless but not void of form, they definitely occupied space, they screamed with color (red) and shape (round) and size (small), and their virtues included things like delicate, gentle, passionate, giving, feeding, and healing to others. Wow. What blessed little things simple berries are. It's like they want to be eaten, so they make themselves bright red to be seen by all the creatures on Earth, and they remove all barriers likes shells and peels and skin or fur so that they can be instantly consumed. Nature's fast food. Their vulnerability is what helps them achieve their life purpose.

I began to giggle with delight and the intensity of such a simple act, the act of really paying attention to something, giving it your full attention. I suddenly loved these little berries, something we would normally think was meaningless.

"They're adorable!"

Ms. Bernadette beamed. "You are a fast learner. We shared many lives, you and I, but the one I can tell you about was made apparent to me during the years of my mental breakdown.

THE RESCUE OF DEMISTRATH

"It was a hidden time in European history, now called the Dark Ages or the Middle Ages. After the fall of the Roman Empire, the continent went dark, in regard to records and knowledge. It was seen as a time of supposed decline, culturally. The idea was perpetuated by religious men and scholars but in reality, the Dark Ages was a revival of the old ancient arts: intuition, midwifery, alchemy, masonry—think of all the building of the great cathedrals. Matrilineal wisdom was again honored and succored. Convents, abbeys, monasteries, and mystical spirituality were thriving. Oral and practical traditions and rituals dominated, and so there were fewer written records. This was the era where we shared one significant lifetime, Eva."

At this point, Ms. B. paused. I was standing completely still with my eyes linked to her face, soaking in every word she spoke. My body was surging with conviction, resonating with everything she said. My body felt heavy and almost ached for knowledge. I just needed her to put everything into words. My head was about to split. Instinctively, we reached for each other's hands.

"Eva, we were sisters then, twin sisters, born in Scotland to an earl, who already had enough daughters, so he handed us into the keeping of the Druids in the forest. The Druids had been driven from the Isle of Iona by the Christians. We were trained and apprenticed in the Druid ways to later become priestesses for the ruling Earl of Perth, in Alba on the river Tay.

"As twins, we were considered to be even more powerful and sacred. We became especially astute in predicting the future. The method we used the most was scrying, gazing into a bowl of holy water. It was around this same time that Demistrath was coming into existence in a parallel dimension, in an area of Western Scotland. During this lifetime as priestess twins, the fairy folk and the humans coexisted in a shared wooded realm. And then something happened. The earl's land was raided. The castle where we lived was overcome by the marauders, probably some fringe Viking tribe. It was horrible, the destruction, the assault, the killing. The fairy folk disappeared from the area, their magic still strong. They were skilled at hiding and camouflage and managed to escape the pillage.

"Here's the sorrowful truth. We had foreseen an enemy encroaching to our region through our readings. But you and I were at odds with the interpretation and disagreed on the details. At the earl's council, the debate delayed the preparations, and thus the attack was even more deadly. One of us lived, and one of us died in the attack. The one who lived escaped to the Druid's lair but was stripped of the priestess duties and sequestered for a life of servitude. Eventually, the fairy folk from Demistrath offered a refuge, and so the remaining twin crossed over to their realm, never to return to the human world."

Bernadette paused. I felt my heart sinking. "Do you know which of us . . . ?"

"I don't, Eva. And it doesn't matter. It was many centuries ago. We have surely paid whatever dues the cosmos required. The point is, here we are, reunited in this lifetime, aligned with Demistrath again, in a different way, and they require our help, and we are destined to return the assistance."

I watched as Bernadette suddenly dropped her hands and started to cry, a silent, tearful stream. "I have suffered so in this madness, not understanding what was happening to me, feeling alone and insane and ready to die. I don't understand why it has taken me so long to recall the truth of my relationship with the otherworldly places and people. I have been bereft of a teacher, a shaman, a wizard, if you will, to help me. My parents, for some reason, did not share their knowledge of the occult with me. I'm not sure why. And marrying Mr. Robinson sealed my spiritual death, into the wasteland of traditional patriarchal subjugation. I feel ashamed, Eva, that I let this happen to me."

I gently placed my hands on her shoulders and drew her closer. "It is not your fault, none of it. And it doesn't matter which of us lived or died in that attack. It was the demise of that lifetime for both of us, the end of the priestess years. I've been having bits of memory in the past few days here, Ms. Bernadette, and you have explained it all to me, much more than I could have imagined."

She bowed and started to turn away. I could tell she was tired and now carried the weight of Mr. Robinson's hospitalization to contend with too. "I will find a way to return to Demistrath, Ms. Bernadette. In fact, I just remembered!"

I probed in my pocket for the quartz crystal Mr. Dabbs gave me, quickly explaining the instructions he gave, and guided my mistress—my boss, my friend, and once upon a time, my twin sister—back to the manor house. *Wow!* All I could think right now was *Wow!*

CHAPTER 13

I RODE OFF THE mountain that afternoon with Ms. B. and Mr. Hans, my backpack squashed on the floor of the back seat with my feet straddling it, under the premise of some exams I had to prepare for and take, and I was to be away for a few days. Betsy arched her eyebrow in that "What's really going on?" expression only I could detect but gamely played along with the sending of good luck routine as the willing sport that she was. I was eager to return to Demistrath and would be bypassing my family completely.

I had my college girl look now, my hair loose and floating around my face, just skimming my shoulders in a relaxed afro. As a mixed race girl, I had not started to tamper with my hair using flat irons and pomades and instead going between flat braids or let loose like it was now. My mother seemed to liken loose hair on a black woman to going out in public half-dressed. "Do something with your hair, Eva!" I would think sardonically, *I have. I am letting it go natural.* I had saved some money to buy a pair of stonewashed denim jeans, which I loved with tank tops in the summer and turtlenecks in the winter. Today I had an old pink sweatshirt turned inside out with the sleeves cut off at my biceps and the neck cut out to scoop open below my collarbones. Thanks to Madonna, girls were having lots of fun with fashion. I wove a bright-colored scarf through my belt loops and tied it at my hip. And my sneakers! I found a cheap knock-off version of white Adidas sneakers at the Woolworth store. I liked to be fashionable like most girls, but I didn't need the brand names.

The car dropped me off in Charlottesville near the hospital. It was assumed I would take the Greyhound bus home. Before climbing out of the back seat, I turned to Ms. B., who gazed at me and took my hand and squeezed it. No audible words passed between us, but she telepathed me, "You know how to reach me, like this, no matter where we are. Follow you heart and your instincts, my dear girl. You can trust the Elemental Council members. I will see you upon your return." I squeezed her hand warmly and then scooped up my backpack and hopped out onto the sidewalk on a Monday afternoon in August. I watched as the silver Buick Riviera drove away. I had absolutely no clue it would be my last time seeing Mrs. Bernadette Autry Robinson.

With my backpack slung over my shoulder, containing a change of clothes, a few toiletries, my journal, and a thermos of water, I headed off on foot for the walk to the UVA campus, where I knew I would find secluded wooded areas. I was grateful my community college partnered with UVA for certain things like library research and special lectures. I found a vending machine and decided to grab a few snacks, not knowing when my next meal would be. Peanut butter cheese crackers and pinwheel cinnamon rolls were my favorites. I inserted two quarters to the vending machine for a cup of black coffee. Again, I didn't know what would unfold for me in Demistrath. I sipped my coffee as I wandered off the sidewalk and onto the dirt path into the wooded area. It was warm but pleasant, with a mild breeze whispering through the trees. I started thinking of Mr. Dabbs and letting his face appear in my mind's eye.

I found a small clearing, where the ground was relatively free of growth and featured a layer of detritus matter: leaves, twigs, nuts, pine needles, clumps of moss. I found a sturdy branch and removed any remaining offshoots to create a smoother purposed walking stick, which I used to draw a wide circle in the ground around me. Satisfied with casting a circle, I removed the crystal stone from my pocket and rubbed it gently between my palms and chanted, "Mr. Dabbs, I summon you now," several times.

I found a smooth flat stone on the ground in front of me and placed the crystal on top of it. I closed my eyes and raised my arms up, palms open, like I remembered Ms. B. doing, and breathed deeply, thinking and saying his name.

Then I waited. As I stood, a cascade of critical thoughts spewed into my brain. "You are absolutely nuts, girl. Look at you, how stupid can you be, pretending to have magical powers?" I was taken aback by the sudden negativity in my brain. I could feel a surge of anger rise from my gut and swarm through my heart and then settle firmly in my mind.

"Get behind me, Satan," I hissed.

That was all I said, but the critical thoughts stopped. It was a phrase from my church upbringing, of course, but it was all I knew, and it welled up in me. How dare anyone or anything question my intent and motives? I believed in myself, and armed with the knowledge of my identity, history, and purpose, I returned to summonsing Mr. Dabbs. He would come, I knew it. I just needed to wait and breathe and believe.

I stood still for a while behind the crystal stone. Thoughts of all that had happened to me in the past few days tumbled on a gentle cycle in my head. My heart was alive and trusting whatever came next and was ready.

"Do the right thing, and the details will sort themselves out," a bored voice purred inside my head. A rustle of leaves stirred off to my right, and I saw the flash of a small black animal. A cat emerged from the bushes and sauntered toward me. *Oh my, can this be the black cat from Demistrath?*

"I am. Where is your mistress?" Although the cat was not opening its mouth or anything like that, its voice was audible to my senses, so I replied out loud.

"You're a mind reader too! My mistress is seeing to her husband in the hospital. Who are you?"

"Ah, I am Anastasia. Mr. Dabbs sent me, when he got your call. He is occupied at the moment but asked me to message you to come with me." By now, the cat had walked into my circle and sat on her haunches, beginning to groom her front paw.

"Are you the same cat I saw at the Lughnasa council circle?"

"I am." She stopped washing and turned her yellow eyes to gaze at me. "We expected your mistress to be here too. She is not coming this time?"

"No, she sent me in her stead." I was chagrinned to see the cat lick her lips as she looked away.

"So you travel between realms as well?" I wanted to stall the time, not sure how I felt about this cat.

"I do. I am very old and very skilled. I've lived beyond the proverbial nine lives." And if cats could smile, this one appeared to grin. She seemed very full of herself. Instinctively, I bent down to retrieve my crystal from the ground, but in a flash, she had exerted her front paw and swiped at the stone, knocking it away from me. Her lithe body sat on the ground, with the stone tucked between her extended front paws. I squatted down in front of her.

"Now this stone is very old too and is quite charmed, you must know. It's the Berilig, one of a family of magical stones that have survived the centuries and have aided the Demistrathians in their times of need. We were not sure where it was, so when you used it, we had the precise coordinates."

I was numb. What just happened? I asked the next obvious question.

"Who is WE?"

"Use your head, girl. You are not stupid, that we can tell."

And again, the strange grinning face this cat could make gazed at me. I stared at her in disgust and disappointment. This was not going well.

"Listen, I'm not going with you. Only with Mr. Dabbs." While I was speaking and in my own lightning flash way, I seized the stone back before Ms. Greedy Paws could stop me. I sprung up and leaped out of the circle, my backpack still securely looped over my shoulders, and ran away.

I heard laughing and then a thump on my backpack, and the wicked Anastasia was now riding on my shoulder. I swatted at her and shook her off me. She landed on the ground, and I turned to confront her.

"Get away from me or—"

"Or what, my dear? Do you really think you can outmaneuver me?" She began to pace around me like a shark circling its prey. I was sorting through a file of possible next steps in this absurd ambush by a cat. I started to run again, this time in the direction of the university campus, where a black cat chasing a college girl would surely entail an intervention.

As I ran this time, she did not jump on me from behind, so I increased my speed for all it was worth. The next thing that happened was so unexpected. I fell backward and was in a chokehold by her claws and paws. Somehow she had passed me and pounced from above. Her face was close to mine, and her eyes were fierce, with narrow slits of iris surrounded by a piercing gold yellow.

"Much as I'd love to keep this cat-and-mouse thing going, we are wanted in Demistrath. Hold still, foolish girl." And it was happening again, the swirling pressure, the absence of light, the feeling of being hurled through space, and then the jolting landing. Dimension travel with a cat was quite different from the steady force of Mr. Dabbs. I landed in Demistrath on my butt.

"And you might want to stop thinking of me as just a cat. I'm much more than that! Now follow me. Dev Sinnott is waiting."

It was a dreary afternoon in the sprawling township of the Demistrath valley. We arrived not on the side of the hill as I expected but in a craggy ravine farther down the slope of another ridge, and the view of the distant village showed a completely different side. We stepped through some tumbled boulders and rocks to merge onto a dirt road. To our left, a small stone castle loomed alone, a rectangular structure with a round turret at each corner. To the right, the road led to the village. Gray clouds covered the sky, and a flock of blackbirds passed overhead with caws and squawks and headed toward the castle. I thought about running to the village again, but I now knew Anastasia, the cat, would stop me. I turned my face toward the village and closed my eyes and sent my thoughts toward the Elemental Council. I could see all their faces sitting in Lara's kitchen, and I formed the words "I am here! Help!"

I turned and followed Anastasia along the rutted road toward the castle. I realized I no longer gripped the crystal stone, the Berilig she called it. A plume of panic rose within me. When did I lose it? Probably in the vortex.

"Did you steal my stone?" I hissed at the cat. I was really angry now. She was walking in front of me in silent padded paw steps. She growled in a low, irritated way, the warning growl cats give.

"It's all hopeless for you now, stupid girl. Shut up." Her tone had changed from the taunting bully she was in the woods to a prisoner guard. The panic that had arisen now sunk back down into my stomach as a lump of dread.

I tried to think about the situation and assess what might be going on. My emotions were intense, but I kept steering myself back to rational thoughts. I had to stay alert and logical. I kept telling myself, "Don't let this fear and anger make things worse." I didn't know how the cat got to me before Mr. Dabbs when I summonsed him, so that was a problem. Obviously, going before Dev Sinnott would be another tedious encounter, but I was quite certain I wouldn't be killed. I seemed to be a person of importance in this realm, whatever that may be, and it did feel like something was unfolding. Then there was always the possibility I could be dreaming and would soon wake up to find myself snug as bug at Ferncliff. I chuckled a little at the thought.

My own snicker was audible, and the cat turned to look at me. I was soothed a little by my laugh and decided to just go along with the game, whatever they had planned for me. I had been initiated into such a vastly different outlook on life in the past few days, that "anything is possible" and "we are all connected' were making sense for this game called life—past, present, future, here, there, now, then, me, you, them, us, "all the world's a stage." I was strangely comforted by this knowing feeling and pulled my shoulders back, lifted my chin, and faced the pair of massive wooden doors of the castle.

One door was opened from within, and Anastasia entered, as did I, scanning the room—gray stone floors, firelit torches on the walls, a wooden table with iron bowls of oil burning flames of fire. We passed through this great room to a winding stone circular stairwell and ascended. At the next level, the cat exited the stairwell, which continued on up beyond us, and we came to a room with closed doors. She scratched on them, and footsteps could be heard coming closer inside, and a door was opened.

Again, I followed but this time was startled to see a completely modern room. Executive desk and chairs filled one end, resting on a massive Turkish carpet. The castle windows were unchanged, I guess to appear no different from the outside, but in here, the furniture was modern—stuffed leather chairs and couch, a coffee table with a bronze sculpture, bookcases, and a wet bar.

Dev Sinnott was sitting in the desk chair and turned it around to face me, his hands laced together and holding the back of his head. He was uncloaked and unhooded and sported a short haircut, wearing a polo shirt and blue jeans.

I guess it was Dev Sinnot because I hadn't actually seen his face at the Lughnasa circle. He spoke, and I knew it was him.

"Welcome, Eva. I trust Anastasia escorted you without trouble to Demistrath."

"Not what I expected, but we're here. How did you intercept my summons? I was calling Mr. Dabbs."

"I was hoping for a little more small talk first. You must be wondering why I'm here, and this room is curious, don't you think? But you seem hell-bent on business." He stood and crossed to the bar. "May I offer you a drink? Something to eat? You are my guest now."

"I'm fine. Yeah, I'm not here to socialize, Mr. Sinnott. I was actually abducted by your cat, and I want to get to my friends." I could feel the anger rising again, and I swirled it throughout my body to simmer slowly and not erupt. I had to stay calm.

"I'm sorry you felt abducted." He laughed a bit. He looked to be in his mid-thirties and could easily pass in a city for a yuppie—white male, educated, likes his coffee and his alcohol, reads the *New York Times*, works out in a gym. He was tall and angular with a surprisingly bland face. He could be any ordinary man and blend in easily.

"And your friends will not be seeing you for a while. I have plans for you, and you will be busy for now, with me, here in this castle. We have work to do, actually." His ruse of joviality faded, and he turned with a drink in his hand. "I have a room for you, and you will be provided with food, clothes, and the comforts of home, if you will accept them, which I recommend since we have work to do."

I stared at him, letting his words sink in. "So I'm your prisoner but pretending to be your guest."

"I see you got your smarts back, missy." The cat purred from one of the leather chairs as she groomed herself.

"And I do have a lot of questions for you, so if that is what you call social small talk, let's start."

Dev Sinnott openly smiled for the first time. "Are you sure I can't get you a drink?"

"I don't drink, or I should say, I have not learned to drink, so a soda is fine."

I expected to be ribbed for this as people who learned I had not yet imbibed alcohol at my age found me to be a cultural curiosity. Didn't matter. I always had more interesting things to do.

But Sinnott did not remark on that, and he poured a Sprite in a glass with ice. He walked over and handed it to me, and I could see he had deep-set eyes that appeared almost indigo blue. I felt uneasy by his proximity, and I needed to stay cautious; he was obviously dangerous and not to be trusted at all. *This connived hospitality is a smoke screen, so don't bite, Eva, don't bite.* I could pretend to be the naive girl people seemed to believe I was and see how far that got me into the truth of this man's world. Arrogant men are such suckers for female airheads and flattery.

I sat on one of the leather chairs and removed my backpack, placing it at my side in the chair, my arm still looped through the straps. I sipped at the Sprite. I was thirsty.

"Are you really the late queen's son, or some imposter come here to take over the land?" I asked.

"OK, let's start there! I am Queen Merideth's son. She never really mothered me growing up. She was disappointed I was not a girl, for the royal lineage, you see. I was sent away from Demistrath to a boarding school in your realm, in London.

"My mother had connections to humans, and it got me out of her glorious hair. She never married and tried several times to have a child, lots of miscarriages, a stillborn or two. I'm her only surviving child." He paused and sipped his drink. "That was fun. What's your next question?"

The cat snorted, and Sinnott chuckled back, and I was becoming appalled at their juvenile behavior. I decided to stay serious and ask my next question.

"Why me? What do you want with me?"

This time Sinnott sobered up and set his glass down on the bar. He was still standing and leaned an elbow on the bar, a leering expression emerging on his face. "For some strange reason, you registered on the oracle's board when we were looking for Bernadette Robinson. Not sure why, and that's one thing I want to find out." He stopped then, and a flash of anger crossed his face. He stepped toward me.

"That's enough. I don't like this game. You don't get any more information. Tell me what you know about Bernadette's recent arrival in Demistrath. What does the Elemental Council really want with her? They don't think I know anything, so I played along. They acted like bringing her to Demistrath would appease me or something. They suggested I invite her, so I acted like I bought into the idea. They are such a stupid group of people, don't you think?"

I was momentarily speechless, trying to make sense of what he was now saying. The cat had stopped grooming herself and jumped off the chair and sauntered over to Sinnott. They were both looking at me. I stood, sure to keep my backpack looped over my shoulder.

"Listen, mister, this is not your lucky day then. I can't answer those questions. I was a simple assistant to my boss, minding my own business in the hills of Virginia, and somehow I got swept up into this crazy realm travel and saga I knew nothing about. Ms. Bernadette sent me back alone because she couldn't come this time, but this is all happening so fast I am about twenty steps behind everything going on, I assure you. And now this!" I gestured to him and the cat and swept my hand around the room. "This is so unnecessary. And rude."

I could hear myself spewing this diatribe with a surge of anger not normal to me. An inner editor was selecting each word with split second timing, and I was glad because I didn't want to reveal anything important to him, and I didn't want to lie either. But I would if I had to. He was a strange piece of work. And the cat too.

I figured he would take a swipe at me now. He stepped toward me and grabbed my two wrists and clenched them together in one of his hands.

"I see you are not going to cooperate. And I gave you a chance. I did." He was almost spitting on me with a crazed look in his eyes, and I realized in this instant this man was crazy. I stared back at him, unflinching. He nodded to the door behind me, and I glanced around and saw two forms move toward me. They had been standing still in complete silence this whole time.

Sinnott let go of one of my wrists and spun me around, and my arms were quickly wrapped behind me as if in handcuffs, and I was pushed forward. The two thugs escorted me out of the office and toward the stone stairwell and up to the next floor. I was pushed forward down that hall, taking a small stumble at one point. I was determined not to act like the damsel in distress and kept my muscles firm and my walk solid. One of the thugs stepped toward a closed door at the end of the hall and produced a large iron key to unlock the door. I was pushed into the room, and the door was immediately closed behind me and locked with a distinct clicking sound in keeping with the chunky iron hardware of the lock and handle.

The room was small and sparse—a single cot, a side table, cold stone floor, and a tall very narrow window, letting in a little light but not big enough to climb out of. I went to the window to see what I could see. Not much. I was high up and could delineate the dirt road and some nondescript shrubs and trees but not much else. Oh great. I wondered if this was the room they intended all along to put me in or if my actions determined this outcome. Never mind. Sinnott was certifiably nuts, and I was going to have to be very careful.

I unloaded my backpack and sat on the cot. I noticed a small enamel bucket with a lid and another open bucket beside it filled with water. *Really? I'm a prisoner then.*

I walked to the door and pressed my ear against it to listen. Nothing. Total silence outside. I kicked the door with my foot and listened again. Nothing.

I decided to lie down on the cot and focus my mind and my intention. The room was pleasantly cool, and I started to relax my body from head to toe. I breathed in deeply and began allowing a picture of the Elemental Council all sitting around the kitchen table in Lara's cottage and began reciting their names one by one.

"Dabbs, Lara, Astrid, Festus, Gunter, Egeria, Lurien." I stopped with Lurien, and my mind leaped at remembering Lurien. *Lurien. Where are you now?* I continued to repeat their names and pulling their faces into greater clarity with each name. I added the phrase "Help me. I'm here in the castle." I didn't know if I should try to signal Ms. B. I decided against it; there was probably nothing she could do from Virginia. Before I knew it, I dozed off.

I woke up to a soft cooing sound and turned toward the side table to see a small tan dove facing me with a cocked head, trying to see me from its side facing little eyes. "Hello there, cutie!" I said, ever so grateful for company. The room had darkened a bit, and I realized I must have slept for a while. I slowly sat up so as not to startle my new friend. The dove backed up a few paces on its three-pronged feet and continued to watch me. I sat still and kept my presence calm. "Did the council send you?" I whispered.

The little bird bobbed its head. My heart quickened. Maybe she understood. "Are you here to help me?" and she bobbed her head again. "Does Sinnott know you are here?" I was thrilled and not surprised as she swung her head side to side, indicating a definitive no.

"OK, my little friend, we are in business!" I kept my voice as soft as possible. I rummaged through my backpack and pulled out my journal and a pen. I tore out a little piece of paper and scribbled "Sinnott Castle, third floor, small slit window." I looked through my things and pulled out a red scrunchy hair tie. I slowly moved to the window and placed it in the opening. Back to the slip of paper, I added, "Look for red hair tie." I rolled up the note to the size of a slim cigarette and placed it on the table before the dove, who had been watching me intently this whole time.

"Please, little friend, take this to the council." The dove wrapped her mighty little talons around the note and flitted to the window, and from there, she was gone. I lingered a while longer by the window and sent thoughts of success and rescue to the little bird. Now it was just a matter of waiting. Or so I thought.

CHAPTER 14

THE GUARDS THRUST open my door. "Out, bitch."
I didn't move. "What's this about?" I asked, and one of them stepped in and yanked my upper arm.

"Master wants you."

"Master? You call him master? What are you guys anyway?"

"Shut up. Walk."

They led me to a different room down on the first floor this time. Sinnott was standing in the hall completely covered in his Druid robe and hood. He handed a gray hooded robe to me and demanded I put it on.

"We're going to take a little walk into the village," he said.

I slipped it on and was hustled into a walking formation behind Sinnott and flanked by a guard on each side. We walked in silence on the road to the village. The sun was setting, and twinkling firelight and oil lamps were beginning to come alive in spots all around the village beyond. My mind was still and my senses alert. The hood of this robe was a bit obnoxious, preventing any kind of peripheral line of sight. I pushed the hood back, and a guard said, "Keep covered."

Sinnott turned ever so slightly. "Follow every order and you will be kept safe. Defy me or my men and you will regret it." Then he turned full around and smacked me across the cheek and mouth with the back of his hand. I was stunned, and the smack was stinging all over my face.

I cried out, "You bastard!"

I didn't know where this language was coming from. I was not known to swear hardly at all but reckoned my current life circumstances were so beyond the ordinary it called for atypical language.

We arrived at a stone building that resembled a chapel, and the guards pulled open the doors, and a flood of warm firelight beamed out over us. I heard one guard announce, "All rise. Dev Sinnott has arrived," and my captor stepped through the threshold, followed by me, the guards closing doors behind us.

The full Lughnasadh council was there. I started to see distinct faces as I glanced around the room, searching for the Elemental Council. I didn't see them at first but then realized they were not sitting together but were sprinkled around the room. I found Astrid, and we locked eyes. She showed no emotion. The tension in the air was thick, and hostility and distrust permeated everywhere. The side of my face was still stinging from Sinnott's swipe.

He strode arrogantly to the front of the room and turned around abruptly, the hem of his Druid robe swirled after him. He didn't beat around the bush.

"There has been scheming and conniving behind my back, and I have intercepted the human party from Virginia until I can determine what is going on."

He was speaking quietly, biting every syllable to the point of almost spitting. *Good grief, man, relax a little,* I thought. All this unnecessary drama. I probably should have been more afraid as I peered around the room at the subjects of Demistrath, who remained tight-lipped and tense. Obviously, more than meets the eye was going on in these charades. I was not sure where my bravery came from, maybe because this whole experience still seemed surreal to me.

"Who invited the humans back, and for what purpose? Answer me now!" Sinnott stormed. He pressed toward a poor soul near him and leaned into the poor man, face-to-face.

"Tell me, Lamet, what is going on with this human outsider meddling in our affairs?"

The man called Lamet shuffled and flinched. "I don't know, truly, sir." Lamet briefly glanced at me and then back to the face before him. "P-P-Perhaps she can tell you." Lamet winced as Sinnott slowly reared back and pivoted toward me.

"Quite so, girl. What exactly was your mission today? And where is the old lady?"

I could feel the heat of twenty-five pairs of eyes turn toward me. I stayed mute as he went on. "And what business do you think you have interfering in a realm not your own? American colonialism is alive and well!" He spat on the stone floor at my feet and turned away. He addressed the room.

"Since none of you sissies will tell me anything, I will get to the bottom of this."

He yanked my arm and pushed me toward the door, the two guards folding into rank on either side of me.

"Wait!" a strong female voice sounded from behind. Astrid stepped forward. "Ms. Eva and Lady Bernadette were invited back here by myself and Mr. Festus. You see, we were childhood playmates of Lady Bernadette."

Sinnott stopped and turned around. "What?

Astrid went on, "Yes, as young ones, we stumbled into Ms. Bernadette's realm, in Virginia, many times. We never saw her again until now. We invited her back. Eva comes with her as her lady in waiting."

I was grateful to Astrid for speaking up on my behalf but not sure where she was going with this personal reveal about her childhood connection to Ms. Bernadette. Sinnott seemed exasperated.

"Come on, you expect me to believe this was just a social visit? I knew from the time your group suggested the Bernadette lady come help our realm it was total bullshit. But I was curious where you were going with it. I did a little research on my own and found that Bernadette had been at Rathven and knew about the abuse of our nature spirits and did nothing to end it."

Suddenly, Sinnott stepped away from our little cluster and raised his voice to fill the entire atrium of this chapel. The village council members who were gathered in the room shifted slightly in preparation.

"I am Sinnott of Dev, son of Merideth and the rightful heir to the queendom of Demistrath! From this day on, I abolish the whole village council, and the Elemental Council is stripped of political rights to serve merely for ornamental functions at the eight Sabbat festivals. Anyone who challenges me will be . . ." And here he paused, searching for his next words. The room was still frozen in thrall as this new twist in the drama unfolded. "Will be arrested and imprisoned."

The two guards stepped forward to stand beside Sinnott. One placed his hand on the sharp knife strapped to his belt, and the other fingered a coiled whip hanging from his waist. Sinnott looked pleased at the gesture of his two men. It occurred to me in that moment they were improvising this whole charade, like playground bullies unrolling their twisted little plot for their own entertainment.

I swept my gaze around the room, looking for backup. Astrid and Dabbs were conferring, and others were looking lost, numb, confused. Other Elemental Council members congregated around Dabbs and Astrid. I stood waiting where I had been left by the doors, wondering if I should bolt. Sinnott and his two henchmen grabbed me in their little pack and proceeded to push and drag me out of the chapel. I could hear Mr. Dabbs shouting behind us, "Let her go!" but there was no further effort made as the doors closed behind us, and they were marching me back on the rutted dirt road.

The sun had set, and dusk was falling on the village as the sounds, smells, and twinkling lights appeared, signaling the end of the workday, the warmth of hearth and home. My heart tugged at the picturesque scene before me as a strong hand clenched around my forearm and pointed me in the opposite direction to the castle. I could hear the chapel doors opening behind me now and the sounds of concerned voices.

I wondered what the Elemental Council was saying to each other. I hardly knew them, my allies, or at least that was what Ms. Bernadette wanted me to believe they were. I could tell they meant well but clearly not enabled for hostage negotiations or standing up to lunatics.

It was dark as we approached the castle, but something was different. Small fire circles and tents and piles of gear and the shadowed forms of people setting up an encampment were clustered in the front courtyard. Did Sinnott assemble an army?

Sinnott remained cloaked and hooded in his robe. One of his henchmen announced, "Lord Sinnott, king of Demistrath," and the troops came to a quasi-attention, turning toward our little squad as we passed through the encampment. I would guess about fifty to seventy-five people, many just staring at us, a few gave quizzical looks. Some nodded. A couple of them bowed. They were an ununiformed crew, dressed in varied peasant or gypsy garb, a couple looked like pirates. For a moment, I had to remind myself this was real and not a movie set. Or at least I assumed it was, or the joke was on me.

I was chagrined to be returning to this gloomy castle, still a prisoner of this amateur tyrant, which made him just as scary but in a different way than an actual tyrant. I realized no one was coming to my rescue, so I had better kick my brain back into gear and pay attention. Maybe I could decipher a way of escape. Then it occurred to me I would be spending my first night in Demistrath. Hopefully, no one back home would miss me. They shouldn't. Ferncliff staff expected me to be away for several days, and my family thought I was at Ferncliff.

I looked up at the night sky in hopes of seeing the beautiful stars, but it wasn't quite dark enough, and there was too much ambient light from the fires and torches. Sinnott was detained outside, but my captor with the vice grip on my arm brought me inside and began to lead me to my cell. I pushed my hood back and looked at him further. He was a bulky man, with a haggard look, unshaven, mussed hair like he just crawled out of bed. He was the one with the dagger. Brawn but no brain, I hoped.

"You from around here?" I asked. He peered at me sideways.

"Shut up."

"Come on, man, really? That's all you know how to say? Clearly, I'm not going to hurt you, but see it from my point of view. I'm not from here, and it's pretty confusing. Just trying to figure things out. This realm is much more than Demistrath, isn't it?"

For a moment, he looked less vacant, but his eyes resumed their voidness as he unlocked my cell door. He had obtained the large iron key from a hook on the stone wall near the door. No way to get the key unless I wrestled it from him, and that wasn't going to happen. I'd be squashed.

It was an uneventful night in my cell. Although I asked for food, none came. I was forced to drink some water from the bucket, and even though I called out from my side of the door and banged on it several times, there was no response. It was a long night. For the first time in this strange magical adventure, the curious, intriguing phase was wearing thin, and it began to settle in on me that worse than something happening next was the possibility nothing would happen. I fidgeted all night long, restlessly dozing, going to stand by the window, hoping, waiting for something to change, to happen. Time just droned on, leaving a girl trapped in a castle tower, with no rescue by a shining knight on a horse, or by a dragon, or by a fairy, or from a magical godmother, or by a royal kiss.

CHAPTER 15

T HE ELEMENTAL COUNCIL had rushed to gather in Lara's cottage following Sinnott's pronouncement in the chapel. Mr. Dabbs was helping Lara set out tea as her hands were shaking badly. Gunter was more prepared tonight and produced a bottle of wine safely nestled in a reed casing and poured a small tumbler full, handing it to Lara before pouring one for himself.

"Where's Lurien?" Egeria said as she pulled herself up to the table and poured some tea. "I haven't seen our guardian all evening. Now's the time we could really use some protective strength."

Astrid joined her, looking more distraught than usual, her impeccable demeanor slightly undone by the harrowing turn of events in the chapel. She unrolled a small paper note and flattened it on the table. "I received this note earlier and was going to relay its contents after the village council meeting, when Sinnott . . ." her voice trailed off as Gunter reached for the note and read it out loud.

"Sinnott Castle, third floor, small slit window. Look for red hair tie." Gunter looked up. "How did you get this? When?"

Astrid was bereft. "My courier pigeon brought it to me, right before the meeting started. I came straight away to the meeting and hoped to pull you all aside as soon as it was over. Then Sinnott barged in with Eva and, oh my!" She closed her eyes and shook her head. "Is it too late?"

107

Mr. Dabbs was pacing behind the group seated around the table. "I was feeling very restless earlier this afternoon. A nagging feeling. I wondered if Bernadette or Eva might be signaling me. But there was nothing precise to go on. I should have followed my instincts. It's my fault!"

Gunter's face was deep in thought. "Dabbs, how exactly do you get signaled from the human world?"

Mr. Dabbs stopped his pacing and looked at the group. Not being very tall, he saddled onto a chair and placed his hands on the table. "It's more telepathic. I hear a voice in my head of the person beckoning from the human dimension."

"And you say you did not hear anything clearly today? Do you think Eva tried to call you, or was she hunted and caught by Sinnott's team without her knowledge?"

"I believe I was picking up some human distress now that I look back on it, but at the time, I didn't have enough to act on."

Astrid gently imparted, "Your travel intuition is rarely wrong, Dabbs. There is now another force stronger and more precise with a darker agenda, and it could be overpowering yours."

Mr. Dabbs was intently wracking his brain. "When Bernadette called the first time, I could hear her signal clearly. It was of a frequency in line with the priestess or goddess. I have only heard it a couple times in my service. When I was apprenticed in the mystical arts, only a few of us were able to access the frequency." He paused, and the council continued to listen in silence. "There is something I need to tell you. I had a feeling Eva and Bernadette would get separated at some point in time, and so I gave Eva the Berilig stone, knowing she was so new to the mystical, and I could see how essential she is to Bernadette. I pray it has not fallen into the wrong hands."

With that, Mr. Dabbs bowed his head on his hands. Egeria stood in front of her teacup. She placed her palms together. The council stirred and looked at her, waiting. "You know I can find things, detect where they are." She rubbed her palms together again. "I cannot find humans, but we already know where Eva is detained.

I can find water, rocks and crystals, medicinal herbs, and certain organics in the soil. I will search for the Berilig."

A gentle wind of energy began to awaken in the council, and they chimed in together with the words "And so it shall be."

Gunter stood and placed his hands on the table. "I will lead a small delegation to the castle to reason with Sinnott. At the very least, it will buy time." He nodded to Astrid and Dabbs. Again, the council chimed, "And so it shall be."

Festus stood. "I will go find Lurien in the woods. We will hatch a plan." The council chimed, "And so it shall be."

Lara remained seated, looking forlorn. "I don't know what I can do," she lamented. "Stay by the hearth and make tea?"

Astrid pondered. "You keep the safe house safe. Use your kitchen spells and cast a circle around this sacred hearth. We will need a place to congregate. Make it strong with protection, Lara."

The Elemental Council was all standing now, some small, some tall, male and female, young and old, bound together by a long ancestral history, by friendship, by cosmos and planet, by knowledge of good and of evil and understanding it was all for a sacred purpose.

Together in sacred unity, they spoke "And so it shall be," and with that, they parted ways to ensue on course to the rescue of Eva and ultimately to rescue Demistrath.

CHAPTER 16

FESTUS, NOW IN his eightieth decade, was still spry and nimble. His species of woodland fairy lived longer than humans, dwarfs, or elves. Astrid was also a fairy. They were a minority now in Demistrath, their ancestors having arrived centuries back at a time when fairies were losing much of their ecosystems to human encroachment, and they came to Demistrath as refugees. It had been hard for immigrant fairies to adjust to a village life back in the day, but they did for survival purposes and were soon recognized by the villagers for the special contributions of wisdom, mystical arts, crafts, and play. Festus and Astrid were cousins from the same nest.

They had never mated or married, a custom of other species that was least practiced by fairies, and procreation was accomplished much like the birds and reptiles through the laying of eggs in an external womb or nest. Because this form of childbirth was viewed as primitive and subhuman, fairies kept procreation and lineage a tightly secretive and private affair. Fairy offspring were so busy at play and exploration by nature, and less self-absorbed than humans, they rarely elicited from their elders details of their birth stories, preferring instead to explore, experiment, and frolic in curiosity.

Festus was trained by the village as a carpenter, and his skills progressed from rudimentary furniture and cupboards to items with finer detail and size such as carved chests, finely curved goblets, cups, bowls and plates, tool handles, and even jewelry and other ornamental adornment. He had even built all the drawers and chests for herbs and medicines now lining the walls of the village apothecary. He mostly found or harvested his wood from the land and was extremely familiar with the Demistrath woods. He knew exactly where to find Lurien.

In a particularly dark and dense area of the spruce forest, there was a clearing at the base of a ridge and far off the beaten path. Villagers just didn't pass this way. Even animals and birds rarely traversed these coordinates. And yet it was not that far from the village, a forty-five-minute hike on foot. It was a black hole of sorts, where one could disappear and not be found because of its blatantly hidden position. The mountain ridge itself adjacent to the clearing was filled with a vast network of caverns. For centuries, it had been the hub of the guardians of Terragon.

Festus had always liked Lurien, who was assigned by the guardians to protect Demistrath a decade ago, and whoever served as the protector automatically sat on the Elemental Council. Festus couldn't remember the last time Demistrath had to seek out the help of the guardians, having lived in peace and neutrality for so long under Queen Merideth.

He neared the clearing, after leaving the footpath a while ago, and made his own way through the plants and trees, grateful for his strong directional intuition. He was careful not to disturb the area, and being small in stature, he could move nimbly, leaving less wake behind him. As he stepped into the clearing, Lurien was standing there, waiting for him, a single shaft of morning light starting to illuminate the ground.

"Welcome, Festus. They have sent you then. What was decided?" Lurien gestured toward a seating area, logs and tree stumps arranged in a circle around a rock-lined firepit. Festus was grateful to sit after the exertion of his hike. Lurien presented him with a handled mug of cold water and sat across from him, long legs bending gracefully so as not to crowd Festus on the adjacent stump.

"Greetings, Lurien. Yes, there was a terrible turn of events last night with Sinnott. Somehow he has captured Ms. Eva, and we don't know where Lady Bernadette is, but she is not with them. He brought Eva to the village council meeting last night, as a prisoner, along with two of his henchmen. He announced his reign, as heir and son of the queen, and said he abolishes the councils, and anyone who opposes him will be arrested and imprisoned. I spied on the castle last night. He has amassed a motley army of hired thugs and lowlife, looks like could be one hundred or so. They are encamped outside the castle."

Lurien's eyes gleamed with anger, head shaking slowly in disgust, looking down at the ground. "Brazen bastard. I never liked him." Looking up swiftly at Festus, Lurien said breezily, "So the council has given the go-ahead?"

"Yes, whatever it takes. But, Lurien, be careful. Gunter is going today to the castle with Dabbs and Astrid. They will try diplomacy first."

Lurien sighed. "That will have no effect, but good luck to them."

After a brief silence, Festus asked, "What is your plan? Demistrath is not accustomed to violence, much less battle. The people need to be warned, or they may get in the way."

"No, we cannot warn the village. Sinnott must be caught off guard. But the fact that he's forming an army complicates things." Lurien stood and looked back toward the opening of the caves. "We must get the girl out of the castle before we capture Sinnott." Lurien placed a gentle hand on Festus's shoulder. "I will send a scout on ahead for the extraction, but, Festus, you must not speak of any of our plans to anyone. Not even the council. Be assured, I will apprise you if assistance is needed."

"How will I know what signals or signs are yours?"

"You will recognize them. My sign is a feather."

Festus lingered and watched as Lurien gracefully swung the quiver of arrows over one shoulder, fluidly grasping the bow in another hand, and then let out the sharpest, most piercing whistle in a burst of three short notes. Festus was smitten for a moment by the elegant, strong figure of Lurien, who, at that moment, turned one last time to Festus, the lock of silken brown hair parting across the eyes, which fastened steadily on Festus. "Travel home safely, and remember, tell no one."

A young guardian emerged from the cave dressed in sections of armor made of leather and padding, armed with a bow and arrows, and several daggers fastened conveniently on different areas of his body. He spoke briefly with Lurien, giving a slight salute, and dashed off into the woods in the direction of Demistrath.

More guardians emerged from the cave similarly dressed; some were male, some female, some like Lurien, could not be discerned with certainty on their gender. Festus pondered the guardians, whom, in his short life, he had rarely encountered, or even thought much about, as Demistrath had existed in such pleasant and pastoral peacefulness. The villagers in general knew about the guardians, for they would enter the village at seasonal festivals and sometimes take part in the parades. Their swagger and pomp was exciting to behold by the artisanal villagers, and youngsters would often mimic the guardians in play. A good bit of flirtation would occur among the young villagers with the guardians, which elicited plenty of ribbing and laughter among the older folk toward the younger.

The band of guardians stood in attention before Lurien, listening to orders. Festus realized they were speaking another language and knew it was time to make his departure.

Festus, feeling small and ordinary in the presence of these magnificent creatures, also felt grateful for their protection and apparent willingness to take up arms to defend Demistrath, to which they really didn't have any heartfelt ties. Festus realized how provincial he was in his life experience, with the arrival of humans, and now the guardians, to their mundane but happy little corner of the world. These outsiders brought with them other worldly knowledge, experience, and sadly, trouble as well. Probably more trouble than Demistrath might be able to bear. His heart felt heavy as he trudged into the woods.

He was pondering Dev Sinnott. Festus saw him up close last night in the council hall. He was tall and humanlike, and this confused Festus. If he was the queen's actual son, he did not inherit her features or physique. Of course, he was not aware the queen had a son, and if Sinnott's story was true, that she sent him away to London to study, in the human world, perhaps that was where his father was from. Why would Queen Merideth do that? Have a child by a human? Genetically, the Druids were the most closely aligned with humans and shared many similarities. But the Druids existed in this realm, while humans existed in the other realm or dimension. Festus could ponder these things better than most as he had traveled between realms on quite a few occasions in his life, as a child and later as a grown man, both times to visit Bernadette, in Virginia and later in Northern Scotland.

He had a nagging feeling Dev Sinnott was a sham, a scammer, and this bothered him so much as he knew the Demistrathians were gullible and simple in many good ways.

Sinnott was wolf among sheep. And he was about to hunt and plunder the innocent for his next meal.

CHAPTER 17

A TRIO OF FORMS walked together from the village toward the castle at the start of the day. The sun had entered the morning sky, and Demistrath was slowly waking up to another day of commerce, market, and trade. It looked like any ordinary day, but the hearts of the three walking toward the castle were heavy, anxious, and silent. Gunter was a Druid and therefore the tallest of the bunch. Astrid descended from the fairy folk, but her bloodlines now contained dwarf as well; her wings were tiny and folded against her back and did not function for flying. Mr. Dabbs was mostly dwarf, and he and Astrid stood about waist high to Gunter. All three were wearing a felt stoll around their necks and draping down in front to signify their visit as official to the Elemental Council. Each stoll was handmade and embroidered with colorful threads depicting symbols of earth, nature, and the celestial realms. Beads and tiny trinkets made of the elements wood, shell, metal, and feathers were arranged across the panels draped in front. Each stoll was unique and fit its wearer.

"Let me start with the talking," Gunter said as they could now see Sinnott's army assembled in the sprawling open space in front of the castle. The trio was quickly spotted, and a shout penetrated above the slow-moving fighters who were still mostly passed out from a night of heavy partying.

"Halt! Who goes there?" A scraggly and rotund sentinel was walking toward them with a spear in his hand, his metal helmet slightly askew. He was squinting into the morning sun as his eyes slowly focused in on Gunter, Astrid, and Dabbs.

"We are from the village Elemental Council, here to speak with Dev Sinnott," Gunter asserted with a steady voice of authority.

"Ha!" said the sentinel as he spat on the ground. "He's not taking social calls right now. As you can see, we are getting ready for an acquisition and merger. I think that's what he called it." The Sentinel struggled with the words, clearly unfamiliar with the vocabulary.

"What you mean is a hostile takeover." Gunter continued, stepping purposefully a little closer to the guard. "We will meet with your leader. Make it happen, chubby, or I will." By now, they were face-to-face, and Astrid and Dabbs could tell the guard momentarily flinched. Gunter put his hand over the guard's hand, where it clenched the handle of the spear, and pushed it down slowly so it pointed to the ground.

"Take us there. We are unarmed and pose no threat."

A runner from the castle suddenly dashed up to the scene. A few other soldiers were wandering up to see what was causing the commotion. The runner was a young adolescent kid and took his job very seriously. "Lord Sinnott says . . ." He paused and panted. "To let them in."

The sentinel rallied himself and blurted, "But how does he even know they came?"

The runner looked startled and then seemed to recover from his instructions. "That is top secret for security reasons." The boy recited and then looked pleased with his performance.

Gunter didn't miss a beat and gave a groan of impatience, pushing past the sentinel and the kid and striding confidently toward the castle doors. Dabbs and Astrid followed close behind, Dabbs taking a protective position slightly behind Astrid to maintain her safety. At the castle doors, two guards let them inside, where Gunter almost stepped on a black cat who had sauntered up to greet them, the shift from bright daylight to the damp darkness inside the castle temporarily creating vision difficulties.

"Watch it, buffoon!" the cat meowed. Only Astrid could hear the cat's words. Without telepathic gifts, the men only heard the feline wail.

Astrid knelt closer to the cat and said, "Where is she? Where is Eva?"

The cat stared back. "Me to know, you to find out!" she said coyly, turning and walking toward the stairs.

Astrid sighed and followed, with Dabbs and Gunter falling in line. Before they could be escorted upstairs, the tall draped figure of Sinnott was coming down the stairs. The cat stopped abruptly, as did the visitors, and formed a small waiting crowd for the castle master to descend. Dev Sinnott was wearing his hooded robe. He stood at the foot of the stairs and planted a hardened stare at the visitors.

"Uninvited guests. Always a pleasure." He sneered. "I thought I'd just stop you right here and get this over with."

He dramatically clasped his hands in front of his waist and fingered a large signet ring. "What on earth do you want?"

Gunter, undaunted, stepped forward. "We come representing the Elemental Council of Demistrath. We come in peace. We are here to negotiate a mutual understanding between yourself and the county regarding your official position and duties."

Sinnott responded exactly as the three expected he might. In a fit of irritability, he waved his hand in dismissal. "Nothing to discuss, nothing to discuss." His two bodyguards firmed up their posture on either side and fiddled with their weapons. "Now remove yourselves from the premises, or my guards will."

Gunter didn't move. "Lord Sinnott"—he now bowed dramatically—"allow us to assist you then in your installment as our leader and make this a peaceful transition."

Smart man, Astrid thought, beholding Gunter's diplomatic skills. Mr. Dabbs was agitated, not recognizing the ploy Gunter was using. Astrid gently squeezed his arm between them, beckoning him to wait.

Sinnott jerked his chin up, lowering his eyes down to view his visitors over the bridge of his nose. "That's better. That's more like it." He suddenly clapped his hands in command and called forth to his minions. "We will have our first cabinet meeting, right here, right now, around this table." He gestured to a large stone table surrounded by wooden benches and chairs. A bowl of oil burned in the center, and a shaft of morning light beamed a rectangle of sunshine on the table. Dust mites danced in the light shaft. Sinnott took a seat at the head of the table, and his two thugs began to seat themselves on either side. He brushed them away, and they returned to their standing positions, on point. Sinnott gestured to Gunter, Astrid, and Dabbs to seat themselves, smiling disdainfully as he saw the smaller folk practically disappear on the benches.

Sinnott steepled his fingers together in front of his face. "So what did you have in mind, there, uh, what's your name?"

"I am Gunter, master metalsmith, this is Dabbs, master of travel and air, and Lady Astrid, the village sage."

"You are so formal. It's quaint. But we live in the modern age, now. Don't you get out much?" Sinnott snickered, looking at his guards, who joined in with their own pointless chortles. Dabbs was disgusted and felt impatient. He was about to speak up when shouts were heard from outside the castle. The front doors flung open into the great hall, and several of the army guards tumbled inside.

"Your majesty! We are under attack!"

CHAPTER 18

I WAS STANDING AT the sliver of the window in my cell, listening and straining to get some clue what was happening outside. I was stiff and sandy eyed from a night of intermittent sleep, and I felt achy in my womb and sore in my legs. I had continued to dream feverishly of vivid ancient lands of the Druids and Celts, fires burning in the fields under full moon and stars, the smell of roasting boar and lamb revolving on open spits, jugs of wine and ale passed and poured, skirts hoisted in dances and jigs, and lovers embracing, rolling around on the ground in beds of leaves and hay. Images of rough sex and squeals of pleasure. I felt rather shocked at the frank lewdness and wondered where I was getting those images in the dreams. Sometimes dreams were quite unsettling. I was more spectator than participant, almost as if I was watching old movie reels of a family history. I realized ruefully I had grown accustomed to regularly and consistently being thrust into past lives, inter-dimensional travel, and voyeuristic journeys in dreams and trance states. My recollection of my simple life back in Virginia and my job as Ms. Bernadette's assistant seemed like the dream.

I heard the metal key jam into the cell door, and I turned to brace myself for the brutish guards. Instead, the door opened, and a flash of green and indigo appeared before me, an arm outstretched and a strong hand held open, palm up, blue eyes flashing, and a steady voice, saying, "Come, hurry, follow me."

Lurien! I was completely disarmed, and for a second, I just froze. A hand reached for mine, and I felt the tug forward. As I stepped toward the door, Lurien's arm circled around my waist, while the other hand grabbed my backpack off the cot, and in a partial spin akin to a dance, I was twirled out of the cell and into the dark hallway.

We dashed down the hall and turned a corner, with me having no idea where we were in the castle or where we were going, but Lurien seemed certain. Lurien was pulling me along by the hand. I could see the quiver of arrows and bow slung over my rescuer's shoulder, the braid of hair swooshing around the neck. Lurien turned to face me. "You will have to jump from this window, but the guardians will catch you. We have no time. The soldiers are coming!"

I just stared into Lurien's eyes, and for a moment, Lurien's face clouded with distraction as we gazed at each other. I could feel the warmth and intense energy from Lurien's lean and muscled body. Then with a rousing swoosh, Lurien placed me in front of the open window and lifted me up on the sill. I stared down to the ground below, and four guardians gazed up at me. My backpack suddenly flew past me and down below, elegantly caught by a pair of upstretched arms.

"You'll be fine. Just stay close to them," Lurien murmured into my ear, and then I was pushed confidently out the window and was falling into the outstretched arms of the four guardians. I was bundled into a web of arms and shoulders below and placed feet first on the ground. We were swept along in a sprint away from the castle and into a nearby wooded area.

Shouts of "Stop them!" sounded from behind. Three of the guardians turned to face the marauders, while the fourth stayed with me, pushing me down behind a craggy boulder.

It was broad daylight, and I was still trying to register what was happening. My guardian pushed me farther down behind the rock in a painful ball as the sound of gunfire blasted around us.

"Christ," the guardian hissed, "they have guns!" I could hear the other guardians level arrows at the assailants as shouts and screams parlayed around the area. Battle seemed to break out in several patches close by and further away. "We've got to get you out of here," the guardian said. "Keep your head down and hold your pack up. It may shield you." With that, I was dragged once more into a stooped run from the boulder deeper into the woods. We hurdled through the thicket of ground cover, and the guardian came to a dead stop and let out a shrill whistle. To my surprise, a bed of leaves and branches lifted up as a hidden trap door, and I was pushed down into the ground as the door closed behind me, the guardian remaining outside, ready to fight.

I crawled on hands and knees down a sloping gravelly ramp into the underground darkness, seeing a glow of soft light ahead. A silhouetted figure emerged from the glow. "This way!"

I obediently followed, able to stand now, and was led around a corner to an open cavern room, where oil lamps dimly illuminated the area. A firepit burned. As my eyes adjusted to the low light, I saw the figure of a woman, not dressed in guardian uniform but instead in a simple linen tunic, belted by a strap of leather holding a sheath and knife.

The woman looked at me with a steady gaze. "You are not from around here. Who are you?" She was staring at my clothes, blue jeans, and sneakers.

I paused. "My name is Eva. I am a friend of the Elemental Council, but you're right, I am from the human world. I was captured by Dev Sinnott's cat and brought here, held as his prisoner, until the guardians rescued me. Who are you?"

The woman reached for a flask of water and offered it to me. "Are you hungry? I'm Hestia, keeper of the hearth. I tend to the guardians and provide herbal medicine."

I gratefully drank the water using my finger to wipe the drips from my mouth. "Do you live here in this cave all the time?"

"Here and back at the clearing too. There's an underground tunnel that connects several storage caches with hidden trap doors such as the one you came through. The guardians have secretly patrolled and monitored the queendom for centuries, usually unbeknownst to its citizens."

Hestia unwrapped a wheel of firm yellow cheese and sliced off a wedge with her dagger. She placed it on a roll of bread and handed it to me. My hands were dusty with grit and soil but never mind, I accepted it gratefully.

"Eat, child. You are famished." With that, she sliced an apple from a bushel basket and handed the slices to me, which I devoured with gratitude, unable to remember when I last ate.

We both heard the shrill whistle again and the rustling sound of the trap door opening and boots crunching on the slope of gravel. "Wounded coming!"

Hestia was already rounding the bend and escorting two guardians carrying a slumped body, lowering the victim to the floor. "Gunshot to the stomach. We are not armed for this battle." They both took off again.

Hestia quickly began pulling back the bloody clothing around the stomach area. "Eva, bring me that bucket of water." I looked frantically around and saw it, also grabbing a lamp off the floor and holding it above the wounded guardian. Hestia sponged off the wounded area and then turned him on his side to peer at his back.

"It did go through, which means we don't know what internal injuries were caused. I will compress the area and hope to keep any infection at bay until we can get him to medical." The victim moaned a bit, and Hestia instructed me to try and make him more comfortable while she gathered the hot herbal compresses and gauze bandaging.

I shifted the young guardian to rest more naturally on the floor. He was smooth-skinned, lean, and strong, wearing the same green and indigo garb, which I realized was their uniform. Hestia swooped in with her compresses, and I watched as she administered the herbs into his wound and wrapping it with gauze. I was relieved to see the bleeding had subsided.

"We will transfer him to the stretcher. I will send for help from medical. I suspect we will have more coming."

I continued to help Hestia as five more wounded were brought in over the course of the next hour. It pained me to see these beautiful people injured, all for trying to protect the innocent villagers and me. I wondered how the council members were faring, and then a flush of relief filled me as I realized I was not Sinnott's captive anymore.

One of the wounded, a buff blond woman who looked to be about fifty years old, was able to speak, and she reported on the battle above. Sinnott's army was using explosives and guns, scavenged from other parts of the land, and the guardians were taking a hit because they were adept at spears, swords, bow and arrows, and other handmade weapons, which historically had been sufficient to hold back enemy activity.

This assault with modern weaponry was Sinnott's doing, the warrior said, and the guardians were eventually driven back to retreat. The castle remained in Sinnott's greedy hands.

CHAPTER 19

LARA HEARD A shuffling sound outside her cottage door and then a slump. She had dozed on and off through the night after spending time casting a circle of protection around the cottage and summonsing the watchful strength of the angels and spirits normally quiet in the ether. She was gifted with clairaudience, "clear hearing," or the sixth sense of hearing messages and instructions and information from the spirit realm. Occasionally, during this morning, she "heard" reports from the angels and spirits about the battle at the castle and the status of her friends. Festus had returned this morning and filled her in on the guardians' plan to storm the castle and rescue Eva, and then he took off, after a simple breakfast from her hearth, to see if he could be of help to the resistance.

Egeria had not been seen since last night, but Lara assumed she was looking for the Berilig stone and staying out of harm's way, Lara hoped. She went to the front window by the door and peered out through the plaid curtains. Something or someone was slumped over on the stone slab stoop of her cottage.

Quietly, she opened the front door and stepped out to the figure wrapped in a large gray Druid cape. She recognized the cape as the same kind worn last night by Sinnott and Eva.

The figure was crumpled in ghastly fashion, and Lara could not discern head from toe. She stooped down to lift a corner of the cape and gasped, throwing off the entire cape from the heap that was Mr.

Dabbs and Lady Astrid, he with his arms wrapped around her in a protective manner. Both appeared to be unconscious.

"Oh no, no, no, no!" Lara cried out and proceeded to disentangle the two bodies and carry them one by one into the kitchen, laying them side by side on the table. She checked their pulses and breath, and finding both, she sighed with relief. Lara could sense the presence of an angel enter the room, and she heard healing hints and instructions.

"Right, they are enchanted, in a spell, but who?" She spoke out loud to keep focused and busied herself gathering her wand and herbs and lighting several candles. She ignited a bundle of pungent herbs and began waving the smoke over her two comatose friends, calling for them to come back.

> Vision of stillness
> Invisible to danger
> Return to yourselves
> Unharmed by the stranger.
> Safe and secure
> Removed from oblivion
> Return to yourselves
> Behold your dominion.

Mr. Dabbs stirred first and then sat up as his eyes popped open. He quickly turned to Astrid while Lara repeated her healing chant. Astrid was older and less hearty than Dabbs. Lara leaned over Astrid, and her heart began to clutch in fear.

"Oh no, no, no, no, no, no!"

"What is it? What is wrong?"

"Ssshhhhhh!" Lara began to chant louder, but this time she placed her hands on Astrid's heart and forehead, closing her eyes to beseech the life force in Astrid to return.

Mr. Dabbs watched in helpless misery as Lara's voice became a soft whisper until finally, she became silent and slowly lifted her hands off Astrid. Mr. Dabbs saw Astrid grow gray and still, while Lara stood frozen before her, turning pale.

She slowly blew out the candles and retrieved a shawl in her living room, which she draped over Astrid's small body. Dabbs was weeping openly, still sitting on the table at Astrid's side, while Lara stood on the other side, wringing her hands and then tilting her head up as if she was listening to something.

"Dabbs, she has left us. Console yourself. She is not in danger. In fact, she is peaceful. The archangel has escorted her home."

Mr. Dabbs was unable to absorb any more soul-threatening drama and stress, having witnessed enough in the past few days to create a tipping point for this gentle, wholesome, loyal Demistrathian. He maneuvered himself off the table, placing a warm hand on Lara's arm as he walked past her and out of the cottage. His eyes landed on a spotted owl feather lying on the stoop and he picked it up, just as Festus came trotting up to the cottage.

"Thank the goddess you are here, man!" Festus gave Dabbs a gripping hug. "The battle is over for today. Sinnott still holds the castle. Gunter took up arms with the guardians. I believe he is OK. Is Astrid with you?"

Lara came to the door. Dabbs just bowed and handed the feather to Festus as he slowly trudged away.

"Leave him," Lara said. "He's had all his heart can take. Come, I will show you." She gestured to Festus, who solemnly held the feather in his two hands and followed Lara into the cottage.

Festus knew without being told what he would find. He was Astrid's cousin, born in the same nest, and their bond was strong. Lara peeled back the shawl so Festus could see Astrid's face. He leaned and planted a kiss on her forehead, placing the feather in her folded hands on her heart.

"Our wise lady has returned to heavens. Oh, Astrid, why have you left us when we need you more than ever?" Festus turned to Lara. "What happened, do you know?"

Lara shook her head. "They were just dumped at my door, I'm not sure by who, and already unconscious in an enchantment spell."

She showed him the Druid robe they were wrapped in. "What can it mean?"

"They must have still been in the castle when the battle broke out. Lurien's sign is a feather. He must have brought them here, wrapped in the robe for smuggling them out maybe."

"Festus, I'm sorry. I tried to save her."

"Aye, you did your best. In the end, we do not direct the course of life and death."

Lara and Festus stood beside the diminutive body of Astrid, who rested in peace on the kitchen table, the life force still leaving a lingering glow on her pale skin. Her bees nest hair formed a nimbus around her face, and her small hands with manicured nails clasped the large spotted feather, an owl's feather, Festus noticed.

"This is a terrible day," Festus said, a pair of tears rolling silently down his cheeks.

Lara placed a gentle hand on his shoulder. "I will make us some tea, my friend."

CHAPTER 20

THESE UNDERGROUND CAVERNS were much colder than the summer August air above. I located my backpack and pulled out my sweatshirt. My jeans and sneakers seemed sorely out of place in this world. A wave of deep sadness overcame me, and I almost fell to the ground. Images of dear souls struggling to live and then having their bodies fall away from them in death played out in my head in flashes of sight. I strained to see where the souls went, but my vision did not let me. The emotions of the dying bodies filled me as I could see guardians who had fought, both now and many centuries ago, trying to save me and the others, but they succumbed. There was fear, terror, resignation, keen disappointment, anger, fury, and longing filling them and spilling into me.

I heard a voice from across the cave call out to me. "Eva, are you all right?" Soon, I was being lifted from where I had crumpled to the ground, and my back was being propped up against something firm. "Get her some water," a voice called out, and then a hand was pushing the hair out of my face. Another voice was saying, "No, wait, she's in some kind of a trance."

A new voice I had not heard before further across the room said, "Who is this girl? Why is she dressed like that?"

"Is this battle about her?" There were other mumblings and softer banter I could not make out, and my trance vision was fading as I came back to the room. Glancing around me, I saw that all was as I had just remembered, about a dozen guardians sitting around in the dim cavern, some standing, many tending to minor wounds and injuries, wiping blood off themselves. The ones wounded most severely had already been carried out on stretchers through the tunnels. Hestia, who had been bustling about with her herbal first aid, was one of the people who had intervened with me just now. When she saw I was back to my normal state, she moved on. I stood and began stepping through the room, holding my backpack in one hand, heading toward the tunnels. Most of them paid me no mind, and I slipped away as quietly as I could. Right now, all I wanted was to find Mr. Dabbs and go back to Virginia. I was so embarrassed to be taking up space in this place where I didn't belong.

I followed the cavern passageway, which was lit by periodic torchlights. Up ahead, two guardians were talking, apparently having met in the tunnel because I could hear them sharing information about the castle battle. As I approached, they both turned to look at me and stopped talking.

"Can we help you, miss?"

"I'm trying to . . . Actually, I don't know what I'm trying to do. Where does this tunnel go?"

"Pretty much anywhere. The hub is on ahead. Check with our commander. We are on stand down orders to remain underground until further notice."

"Thank you." They parted to let me pass. I could feel their eyes following me. I willed myself to keep marching forward with confidence. I had to at least pretend like I knew what I was doing. It seemed essential to staying safe.

The hub was abuzz with activity and sounds of people's voices, the clang of metal being hammered. The medical station was here as well as an eating hall lined with long tables saddled by simple benches. An armory in one corner stashed weaponry and what appeared to be a repair shop. In another corner of this great underground room, several medics dressed in linen robes hovered over the injured guardians, now resting on cots and tables. What looked like CPR was being intensively administered to a barrel-chested warrior. I was standing on the edge of this whole scene, my mind taking it all in.

Then I saw Lurien, intently conversing with several other guardians at one of the tables, pouring over maps spread out among them. All I could do was stare at this person, a deep feeling of longing and allurement holding me fast, unmoving. Probably feeling my pointed stare, Lurien looked up from the maps, fastened intense eyes on me, and then gave a quick word to the others at the table. We both started moving toward each other at the same time until we were face-to-face.

Lurien looked me up and down and smiled. "You are OK then. I'm glad to see." Lurien was just a little taller than me but not much, and I noticed the smooth skin and keen expression on a face so full of strength and knowing.

"I am. I can't believe the awful battle. I'm so sorry for the loss of your guardians and all the injured."

Looking away, a pained expression crossed Lurien's face. "It was much worse than we could have imagined. I take responsibility. I did not dispatch enough scouts ahead of time to assess the situation. Sinnott is more cunning than anyone would have imagined. Come, I want you to meet some others. We are working also on why he kidnapped you and Lady Bernadette had she been with you."

"I can't thank you enough for rescuing me, Lurien. I was just beginning to lose hope." We were walking toward the war table.

Lurien smiled then, and it was the first time I saw a smile. It was breathtaking.

"You were the perfect rescue—no argument, no questions, complete cooperation, even agreeing to jump out of a window. I was impressed."

"You've had a lot of experience rescuing damsels locked away in towers then?" I returned with a little flirtation.

"It's my business!"

I soon learned I was to be assigned a bodyguard or two and kept underground. Mr. Dabbs would be sent back to Virginia to find Ms. Bernadette and make sure she never returned to Demistrath.

The guardians had a couple of undercover spies in the castle, and from what was gathered, Sinnott relied heavily on an oracle for his intelligence. This oracle was not a very old witch versed in prophesy, spells, and foresight, like I imagined. Consistent with Sinnott's mode of operation, the oracle was an electronic device he had obtained in the human world, which, by description, sounded like a cross between a high-frequency radio and a computer. Sinnott had done some extensive research in family lineage and had traced the queen's ancestors back centuries, discovering that Lady Bernadette shared one of the same matrilineal bloodlines as the queen. A chilling feeling ran through me, remembering the ties to Demistrath Ms. B. referred to.

I shifted and sat on the bench. Lurien shot me a glance from across the table. "You all right?"

I nodded and looked back at the maps to shift the attention away from me. "Breathe, Eva," I told myself, letting everything sink in further. The Elemental Council was out there somewhere, and I was to go to them all along, and right now, I felt completely derailed. Did others know of the ancient connection between Lady Bernadette and the queen? No wonder they treated Ms. B. as royalty.

While Commander Lurien conferred further with the war council, their voices fading in the background, I closed my eyes and conjured my thoughts toward Ms. B. It was time to try to reach her. "I am safe in Demistrath," I projected, repeatedly into the mental ether of my thoughts. Images of her face swirled like wisps of smoke and effervescent plumes of sparkling fairy dust in my inner eye. She was smiling, and it seemed like she was waving at me. Then the image was gone, and only the words "Well done" lingered before vanishing too.

I stood and started to ease myself away from the bench and table and was suddenly flanked by two guardians; one was a young willowy thin reed of a teenager, and the other was a short, robust, muscle-bound man with a silver crewcut, both armed with fine Demistrathian weaponry (knives, bow and arrows, a sword in sheath) and silent as mice.

Lurien noticed the flurry and stood, gesturing to the bodyguards.

"Eva, this is Kort and Nemi. They will guard you at all times, but they will not chat or become your friends. However, if they ever give you instructions pertaining to your safety, you are to follow their orders." Kort, the elder of the two, and Nemi stood at attention, and both gave me a slight nod.

"Hello, and thank you," I said back to the guards.

I turned my gaze back to Lurien and saw the distant protector bearing in their face. "Excuse me, Commander, but I wish to return to the Elemental Council. They must be worried about me. Is that possible?"

"Not yet. But word has been sent to them on your safety."

I was then shown down another passageway lined with doors on either side, little single rooms for sleeping. A cotton-batted mattress on the floor with suede pillows and marbled knitted blanket made for a very soft resting spot. The simple room had a braided rug on the floor and a washstand holding a large crockery basin and barrel of water with a wooden ladle hanging to the side. Several folded handcloths were neatly stacked beside the basin. An oil lamp burned on a nightstand. Hanging on one wall as art was a tree branch with many twiggy offshoots laced with feathers and leather cords attaching cockleshells and seedpods, crystals stones, and various rounds of moss. I stood fixated by the wondrous creation. It breathed of the earth and the minerals that ground us. I loved this room instantly and flopped down on the mattress, removing my clothes and my shoes and pulling out the spare outfit from my backpack. The clothes I was wearing would probably have to be tossed. I wanted to bathe. Sponge bathing, my mama called it. I stood at the basin and "sponged" myself off. The water was a little cool at first, but I soon got accustomed to it. A bar of soap helped.

A light knocking on the door froze me.

"Who is it?" I called out.

A little high-pitched voice said, "Room service."

I quickly wrapped the blanket around my body and opened the door a crack. I had to look down. A tiny woman, perfectly proportioned so that she looked like a three-foot-high china doll, was standing in the hall, smiling up at me.

She was pulling a small wagon holding folded clothes, shoes, and grooming and toiletry items. "The commander thought you would need some extra things, coming from another place and all," she said shyly.

I opened the door, inviting her in, closing it behind her and the loaded wagon. I knelt so we could see each other face-to-face. She was completely magical, fairylike, reminding me of Astrid, but even smaller. Ringlets of strawberry blond hair circled her head in a cacophony of layers and made me think of my own hair, and that it probably looked like a bird's nest fallen to the ground. I had left it free and unbraided eons ago when I was abducted from Virginia, and since then, I had been imprisoned by a madman, rescued from a castle, escaped through a battlefield, and tumbled underground. I didn't need a mirror to tell me what my hair looked like! My new visitor seemed to be thinking the same thing as she eyed me with the calculated stare of a hairdresser getting ready to tackle the job with scissors and clippers. "You are indeed a mess!" her voice chirped playfully. "I see you are bathing. That is good. We have fresh clothing for you, shoes, and grooming items. I am told you are called Eva. I'm Dawn."

"Hello, Dawn, nice to meet you. And thank you! How did you get to be underground with the guardians? It seems so out of place."

"That, my dear, could be a long story! This realm has been slowly turning upside down for a while now, but when Sinnott took over the castle, I couldn't just sit back and watch. Much as I loved being a nest grandma, I wanted to help this cause. Demistrath is a special place in all the counties and has been a haven of welcome and shelter for all peoples and creatures for centuries. We are known in the queendom as the neutral safe place."

"Do you know the members of the Elemental Council? They are my contacts here. I was to meet up with them but was derailed by Sinnott and his cat Anastasia, the beast! Have you met her?"

Before Dawn could answer, I continued, suddenly spilling out all the happenings of the past day or two, unable to stop myself.

Dawn listened patiently as she took over dressing me in an outfit I was barely paying attention too but vaguely aware it would make me look more native to Demistrath and not the garish garb of 1980s America. The shoes were delicious on my feet, more like slippers, and now she was doing something to my hair with oil and smoothing a cooling cream on my face. I closed my eyes and shut my mouth and let the silence enfold me like a warm blanket. Next thing I know, I was sobbing. Yes, sobbing, so much so Dawn had to stop her administering of the ablutions and just pet my arm, cooing, "It's OK, honey, you've been through a lot."

I had mixed feelings about these "good cries," as my mama called them. On the one hand, they completely rid me of all the tension and sadness and fears that accumulated, but they were embarrassing if they happened in front of others and, frankly, made it very difficult to breathe. As if on cue, Dawn reached for one of the handcloths and brought it to me to blow my nose. *OK, definitely pull yourself together Eva,* I admonished. My mama used to say the same thing. She'd let me bawl in her lap, and then she'd make me stop. *Thanks, Mama,* I thought, *for teaching me how to recover.*

"You are blessed to have mastered the art of weeping. Most adults are cut off from their tears, I have noticed. Yes, I know the members of the Elemental Council. They have been in place for some time and served our queen well."

"What happened to her, the queen? All I know is she passed on a year or two ago. Was it sudden? Unexpected?"

"No, she was sick for some time. But she did not let it show at first. What some started to notice was that she would make her public appearances much shorter, and the Elemental Council worked behind the scenes to have healers and herbalists tend to her. But in the end, she just fell over one day, and her heart stopped. There was no bringing her back. It was terrible news to the whole queendom, shocking, as you can imagine. We are generally not consumed by mysterious diseases and typically die from accidents, injuries, and natural old age."

Dawn was now finished grooming me and stood back.

"You look truly beautiful and refreshed now, Ms. Eva. The commander has asked me to attend you, so I will be at your beck and call. Your bodyguards are stationed outside the door and will remain close by. A meal will be served soon. I'm sure we will get some news of the situation above. Commander Lurien will provide an update of some kind. Scouts have been coming and going all afternoon with new reports."

I felt a flutter of anticipation return as I stepped out of the room and into the passageway. My guards stirred quickly and stationed themselves one in front and one behind as I walked toward the great room. It was mealtime. The dining quadrant was filling with guardians taking seats at the tables, multiple conversations buzzing. I scanned the room but could not find Lurien. I was directed toward a table and seated, and soon, Hestia saddled up beside me.

"By the goddess, I barely recognized you, Eva! How are you?" Hestia was cleaned up too from her medical work and seemed to be on break. I was extremely impressed with the teamwork here.

"They are taking very good care of me. How are you? You must be tired."

"I am but in a good way. It's been a rough day, but all the wounded and injured have been treated." I could see her better in the light now, here in the great room. She appeared strong and capable, a no-nonsense flair about her, with brown hair and eyes and a quick laugh. She was simultaneously holding forth several bantering conversations with others at the table. I ate the hearty fare prepared for us, and smiled politely, and felt relieved that for the most part, the guardians left me alone. Occasionally, I could see someone glancing at me sideways, but a curiosity was understandable. I reached for the gleaming copper mug set before me and took a swig.

"Oh my!" I blurted as the red wine streamed across my tongue and down my throat. I coughed a little. "I was not expecting wine!"

Hestia peered at me. "Why, what do they drink at your meals?"

"Water? Soda? Iced tea? And a lot of people drink wine too, I guess."

"You are a funny girl." Hestia chortled. "Soda. Iced tea. Those are new to me."

Recovering from the dry taste of the wine, I said, "Well, maybe someday I can share those beverages with you."

A sharp whistle sounded from across the room, and everyone grew quiet almost instantaneously. Lurien strode in, followed by a couple of scouts and some advisors. I could feel Kort and Nemi behind me come to attention. The salute here was a fist placed over the heart. A bevy of salutes went on between the guardians and Lurien. I heard Hestia whisper, "This is the evening report."

One of the advisors spoke first. It was like the evening news without the television. A summary of the battle today at the castle was first. "A total of twenty-six guardians injured and wounded. One casualty. The family was already notified. Sinnott's army was impaired with fourteen killed, others wounded, but with their guns against our swords and arrows, the match was skewed. For now, Sinnott still holds the castle, and his army remains encamped outside. So far, they have stayed out of the village. The people have remained in their homes, with very little foot traffic and all businesses and markets closed early for the day.

"Three members of the Elemental Council initiated a diplomatic mission to the castle this morning: Lady Astrid, Mr. Dabbs, and Mr. Gunter." My ears perked up, and my heart started beating faster.

"They were detained inside the castle by the enemy when the battle broke out. Our commander and first unit breeched the castle, rescued the human prisoner, and were able to secure Astrid and Dabbs, both found unconscious, and their bodies were returned to the Elemental hearth. The word is that Mr. Dabbs recovered, but Lady Astrid did not. We are deeply saddened by this loss today."

CHAPTER 21

I BOLTED UPRIGHT FROM the table, shocked by what I just heard. "I must get to them right away!" I stated firmly. I could feel Hestia try to pull me back down to my seat by tugging at my arm, and a few murmurs filled the room.

Another advisor stepped forward and said, "While we can appreciate your passion, no one is leaving this cave until further notice." A surge of heat pressed at my face, and I could feel the flush in my cheeks. I sat back, looking at my plate. *What's wrong with me?* I wondered.

Hestia spoke. "It's all right, dear. Everyone knows you mean well." I sensed a movement behind me, and a hand landed gently on my shoulder.

"Come with me." It was Lurien. I stood and stepped away from the bench and followed the leader, with Kort and Nemi behind me.

Lurien led me out of the great room and into what appeared to be a sitting room or parlor. A fire danced in a central hearth, and various chairs and lounges were positioned around it. "Have a seat." I sat on the first cushion I saw. "Leave us," Lurien said to the guards, and they exited. It was just me and Lurien, who sat nearby and turned to me. "Eva."

"I know, I'm sorry." I was still looking down. The more I saw of Lurien in action, the further I felt from them. My mind scrambled with their gender. This was a somewhat confusing piece, but a piece that did not matter to me: what mattered to me was that my heart was under attack from a rush of attraction like I'd never known before.

"Here's what I can tell you."

I looked up into the face of Lurien who had become my rescuer and my commander. Good grief. I was crushing hard. Shyness forced my gaze down again until a hand gently lifted my chin and then let go.

"What I can tell you is, we have learned Lady Bernadette shared ancestry with our queen, which made her a threat to Sinnott. We don't know what he intended to do with her, but he got you instead. We also know that you are more than you realize." Lurien paused, searching my face. I waited.

"Our sages have long been predicting that Demistrath would be ruled someday by 'one not of our own,' is how it has been said. At first, we thought it was Sinnott. But some new divining wisdom could be pointing to you."

I shook my head. This was too much. I stood and walked to the other side of the room. I was homesick, in grief, completely enmeshed in a strange land, worried about my loved ones back home and now worried about my new friends here, completely off balance from my feelings for Lurien, and now this. I turned and found Lurien's face across the room, still looking at me from a seated position, elbows resting on knees, hand over hand, calmly waiting.

And then it happened. Ms. B. was talking to me. Inside my head, of course. I could hear her word for word. "Eva, what Lurien says is true. Don't be afraid."

"Where are you? What's happening?" I sent my thoughts back.

"I am fine. Don't worry about me. You must carry on there, in Demistrath. Trust it, Eva. Trust it. Just walk on." A sense of ease started to return to me as I waited to listen for more words, but they stopped coming. I peered back at Lurien, still waiting.

I spoke now to that beautiful person in the room.

"May I call you Lurien, Commander?"

"In private, yes. Not in front of the others."

"Lurien, I do, in fact, know quite a bit more from Lady Bernadette about our connection to Demistrath." I paused. Lurien was slowly sitting upright. "I don't know about what you just said," I continued, "but I have her blessing to move forward here. I don't know how long she will be detained in Virginia, with her husband sick and all. But I am instructed to carry forth here, whatever that means."

Lurien was standing now. "I'm glad to hear it. As we've established, you are an easy rescue, and you take instructions well. Now we'll have to see how well you lead." A picture of myself with a crown and scepter, standing on a platform flashed before me.

"Whoa there, cowboy!" I jested and then giggled when I saw Lurien's confused expression and raised eyebrows. I walked back. "And I will follow the decorum of the governing state here, Commander. I promise."

Lurien smiled and motioned to the door. "And please, Eva, don't try to escape, especially not without me, OK?"

I placed my fist on my heart and said sincerely this time, "I promise." I impulsively raised my hand like a high five, and to my surprise, Lurien placed a palm up against mine, our fingers clasping for a moment, and then released, and Lurien became commander once again.

After that, an industriousness permeated the guardians' underground lair, and everyone was gearing up for what would come next. Lurien and the advisors were hatching another overthrow plan. My first night in the glade, as I learned this place was ironically called in a way to foil its location, was the best sleep I could remember. My little room was like a womb for me, and I felt safe, comforted, and supported. Dawn and I were becoming fast friends. She was so curious and gracious and motherly. She was one of the few single-blood fairies left in Demistrath and was already over three hundred years old, and because she was such a treasure, she lived under constant protection with the guardians. Not happy being idle, she always found something to do, and apparently, nothing was beneath her. She loved to tell stories about her "early years" above ground, living and working among the Demistrathians and then serving as the fairy nest mother and later grandmother, a communal nursery for hatchling fairies. She never had offspring of her own as she found herself too busy caring for others. Of late, she had developed her own take on providing "room service," a human term she heard one time from a passing traveler through Demistrath. In typical Dawn style, she ran with the idea and individualized her services for each person. Everyone loved and revered her, I observed; she was always greeted with cheer and often in affectionate jest, which she would give it right back.

I spent part of day 2 in my room, having my own private memorial for Astrid. I was so grateful for the nature art hanging in my room as it symbolized Astrid to me. Living underground, I missed the sky, the trees, the breezes, the sun, the moon, the starry sky, the smell of fresh air, and the grass, leaves, earth, cool water from a stream. I asked how people stand it down here so long and learned the glade had a large entrance into the woods, and normally, everyone had daily access to the outdoors. Rarely were they sequestered below ground. This was unusual.

Apparently, I was not the only one longing to be outside. By the afternoon, contingents of guardians and staff were given shifts to go outside and take care of whatever business they might have. Some guardians had made connections in the village, some were recruited from the village, so they would normally have homes to go to. However, because of the hostile siege, they were now on active duty and had to stay on the premises. Security was tight. When my turn was granted, I followed a retinue of a dozen others, and we processed through winding passageways into the foyer of a cave with daylight pouring in. My heart sang at the sight.

I wandered into the literal glade, now understanding the name of this guardian headquarters, and walked to the fireless pit and log benches. The surrounding tree foliage was dense, and the trees were packed together in close range with underbrush filling the spaces. I saw a single opening with a footpath into the woods. Otherwise, from what I could see, this open glade was completely surrounded by a wall of nature. Several armed guards were walking the perimeter.

THE RESCUE OF DEMISTRATH

I sat on a bench and closed my eyes, breathing deeply of the air and sensing the warmth on my skin. In the daylight, I could see better the tunic I was given to wear. It was made of an emerald green material with fluttery sleeves past my elbow and a shawl collar I could pull up over my head if I wished. The slippers were russet suede, held onto my feet by suede ribbons that crisscrossed a couple of times up past my ankles. The undergarments were a kind of knickers or pantaloons and a loose-fitting undershirt or tank top. I liked the feel of the clothing on my body. I listened with my eyes closed again to the sounds around me and soon fell into a meditative state. All was calm within me. I liked this world, this place, deep vibes flowing through me. It was a feeling of aliveness I never knew before.

My inner stillness was shattered by a stout whistle, which, by now, I knew meant we were called in for a briefing. I traipsed back into the cave with my cohort, turning one last time to glance back at the woods, taking a mental picture, not knowing when any of us would surface again.

CHAPTER 22

T HE GREAT HALL, as I came to call it, was filling with guardians. Already, Lurien and the advisors were there, huddled around a sweating, red-faced scout who must have run all the way here with news. A seriousness fell upon the room as everyone grew quiet. The "news" advisor stepped forward.

"We have just learned the Elemental Councilman Dabbs made an unauthorized action while in the human world and returned with an unknown human man, who is prepared to assist us with the overthrow of Sinnott. Obviously, we are looking into this and will be vetting the visitor and questioning Mr. Dabbs before further action will be taken. In the meantime, the castle remains on constant surveillance by our rangers. Little has happened there since yesterday's battle, but we will deploy several backup units to join forces with the rangers ready for action. As always, we hope no violent force will be needed, but we will be prepared."

Lurien then stepped forward. "I have selected a special operations team to go with me and address the Dabbs issue. Remain on standby. Those chosen will be notified to meet us in the keep." Lurien turned to leave and then stopped. "This won't take long. We need to go immediately."

The advisors walked to the keep, the name I learned for the room where Lurien and I talked yesterday. My guards, Kort and Nemi, came up beside me where I stood.

147

"You, miss, you are going," Kort said, and before I could utter a word, we were heading toward the keep. Inside the room, a beehive of activity had unfolded, armor and weapons were strewn around, and certain people were being outfitted by a team of assistants. I soon found myself being fitted with a mesh vest and a thick leather girdle around my waist and hips, and my slippers were exchanged for boots. A sheath and dagger were attached to my side, and a long-sleeved leather jacket enfolded around me. A helmet of sorts was placed on my head. I took in the others being suited up. Lurien, one advisor, a scout, and Kort seemed to be the team. Kort was detailed to protect me, Lurien and the scout would take lead, and the advisor would follow. With those briefest of instructions, we were then ushered out of the guardroom, into the passageway, and out to the cave entrance.

As soon as the five of us stepped into the glade, a unit of ten additional guardians gathered in formation around us. I heard Lurien speaking quickly in another language to them. To exit the glade, we had to leave in single file on the footpath. I found myself running at a little trot. I was amazed how naturally I fell into the action here, probably more because of the precise training and movements of the guardians than any credit to my natural ability. Kind of like when you are learning to dance, and you flow so nicely only because your dance instructor knows exactly what they are doing.

Our military retinue never left the woods but trotted along various marked and unmarked paths. I was starting to tire and began lagging a little. I could feel Kort behind me adjust his pace. "You're doing great, my lady. Just a little more." he said between his own pants of breath. And he was right. A new whistle signaled from the front of the line, and we all came to a standstill. The unit of ten split out in every direction around our core team, and the scout moved ahead out of the woods. We waited.

I heard another whistle signal, and Lurien made a hand motion, and we advanced forward where the scout had gone.

We were approaching the back side of a cottage, which I soon recognized as Lara's cottage in the grotto. The scout was holding the back door open and then remained outside as did Kort. Only Lurien, myself, and the advisor entered Lara's kitchen.

I glanced around quickly. Lara, Festus, Dabbs, and Egeria were present. And to my utter surprise, so was Shamus!

The ubiquitous Shamus who kept showing up in Scotland, and then Virginia, and now Demistrath was dressed in what seemed like safari gear: khaki cargo pants, a many-pocketed khaki vest, boots, and a tan pith helmet. *Weird,* I thought. I was probably unrecognizable in my new garb, so I removed my helmet.

"Shamus!" I said.

"Hello, lass, it's me." I was speechless, and the rest of the room remained silent. Lurien and the advisor removed their helmets too.

Lurien spoke next. "Eva, do you know this man?"

"Yes, Commander, I do. He is from Ms. Bernadette's household staff." I glanced over at Mr. Dabbs. "How did you two find each other? I'm confused."

"It's OK, Eva, I'll take it from here," Lurien said quietly. "Please sit down." Lurien motioned to Shamus and Mr. Dabbs and then to me. Lurien took the fourth seat. Lara slid a large tray of tea and tartlets onto the table, but one glance from Lurien and she quietly and swiftly removed it.

"What do you know of our realm, Mr. Shamus?" Lurien began.

"Everything."

"Everything?"

"Yes, Ms. Bernadette shared her knowledge with me before she . . ." He stopped. "We met years ago in Scotland, you see, at Rathven. I was a reporter at the time and looking for a good story."

Lurien turned to me. "Is this true, Eva? Did Lady Bernadette tell him about us?"

I was floored. "N-No. In fact, she told me as recent as Warm Springs that Shamus did not know about all this. I'm sorry, Shamus." I looked at him. "This is confusing."

Mr. Dabbs cleared his throat and said, "After the battle and Astrid's passing, I got a signal from the human world. It was the Berilig stone, Eva, and I went to its coordinates, landing me in

Virginia, to this wooded area not far from many big buildings, and a search party was looking for you. They had a couple dogs. I stayed hidden until they left, and Shamus here, he could see me. He found the stone on the ground, and I learned so many things, Eva, but in short, he said he could help us."

Mr. Dabbs's expression was deep and sad, and he peered earnestly at the council assembled here. "I thought it was as good an offer as we'd get, given Sinnott's army. And their weapons."

I was feeling a deep unspoken weight in the air, of what, I wasn't sure. The advisor was leaning into Lurien's ear and whispering something. Lara was still awkwardly holding the tea tray, with Festus and Egeria standing nearby. *Where is Gunter?* I wondered. Shamus was simply looking down at the table and then glanced at me. His eyes were dark and veiled, giving that poker face he was so good at. What did he have up his sleeve?

"What is your plan of aid, Mr. Shamus?" Lurien was directing the process again.

All eyes were turned on Shamus. "May I?" He gestured to a large dark duffel bag on the floor. Lurien nodded, and Shamus heaved it up, as it seemed heavy, and very carefully laid it on the table, unzipping the top open.

"I understand your insurgent is using guns against your arrows and swords," Shamus started. "I have guns here and ammo. It will help you take back the castle and arrest the leader."

I heard Lara let out a gasp as Shamus pulled out a rifle and pistol. "I volunteer to go on the raid, and I can arm up to seven others. They will need some training, of course."

I was disturbed to see these harsh military weapons laid out on the wholesome table so gently shared by the hospitable Lara. The council members were all eyeing the weapons with doubt and disdain. Dabbs just looked woeful.

"I don't believe my troops could master the use of these weapons in the short time we have, Mr. Shamus." Lurien broke the silence first, staring at the intricate metal contraptions. Even though they were from my world, I had not been this close to military-grade weaponry. I'd seen some hunting rifles at the estate but nothing quite like these.

The advisor nodded in agreement. "We must strike again today, before Sinnott makes his next move. If he infiltrates the village, the war will be on. We have to contain it at the castle and snuff him out. Our guardians are already positioned in the woods surrounding the castle. They are ready to attack. We cannot delay."

Lurien added, "If you want to help us, Shamus, arm yourself, but we will proceed as we are."

It was decided to storm the castle, and I was instructed to remain at the cottage with the four council members, while the rest hustled out the back door, parlayed with the unit waiting in the yard, and off they went. Kort stayed behind to guard the cottage, for which I felt grateful. I was relieved to gather around the kitchen table with my new friends. The tea tray finally landed on the table where it belonged. We conversed rapidly, filling one another in on all that had transpired since the fateful day I was intercepted by a black cat and locked in a dungeon.

We cried together over the loss of Astrid. Lara took me to a back bedroom, where she had laid Astrid's body, covered with a sheet. She was so distraught that the body could not yet be returned to the fairy glen for a respectful burial. Dabbs explained what happened in the castle. Before they could enter into negotiations with Sinnot, they were overrun with shouts of the attack on the castle. Chaos ensued. Sinnott disappeared up the stairs, and Gunter leaped up to shield Dabbs and Astrid from harm. As the one-on-one fighting intensified in the castle great hall between the guardians and Sinnott's soldiers, Dabbs said Astrid conjured a spell to feign death, hoping it would appear they were both finished, and thus keep the enemy from capturing them, or noticing them, or getting any other nefarious ideas what to do with them. Gunter disappeared into the fray as Dabbs and Astrid fell to the floor in the corner.

"I can't tell you what happened after that. It was Lurien who brought us here, but why the commander left the fight, I don't know. Maybe by then, the guns were pushing everyone back."

The table conversation fell silent for a moment. Egeria made a clinking sound with her spoon on the china teacup as she stirred her tea. All my senses were alive, keen, and highly tuned. I could hear, see, smell, and feel a universal motion swirling around us, and then I sensed the arrival of others enter the room. I closed my eyes and felt or recognized the spirit of Astrid and also Bernadette. Both of their energies were precise and full of love and kindness.

"Dear Eva, don't be alarmed." This was the presence of Astrid speaking. "Please let the others know I am well, safe, and happy, and they must not be dismayed about my passing. Especially Mr. Dabbs. It was not his fault as he feels it is." She paused. I could feel the presence of Bernadette, but her voice was silent.

I opened my eyes and peered around the table at my friends, who had all fallen into their own private reveries.

"Everybody," I said, "I can feel the presence of Astrid and Bernadette in this room right now. Astrid wishes to tell you all she is fine and not to suffer from her passing. Especially you, Mr. Dabbs. Astrid assures me you are not to blame in anyway."

The council all looked at me with a mix of surprise and appreciation.

"Ms. Eva, you have the gift of a Polaris!" Mr. Dabbs exclaimed. "Is there more?"

I listened quietly and closed my eyes again. I could feel the love of Astrid just beaming at me and everyone in the room. "Can you feel her love?" I asked out loud. There were some affirmative murmurs from the council. I then sensed Ms. Bernadette stirring. I mentally leaned in toward her and phrased my question. "Is everything all right?" I queried and waited.

The energy spirit that was Ms. Bernadette began to fade away. "No, wait, Ms. B.!" I said out loud, but it was too late. She was gone. My eyes fluttered open, and I was taking some deep breaths.

The council had gathered around me, asking me if I was OK. Only Mr. Dabbs remained seated where he was, still looking miserable. I zeroed in on him. There was something he was not telling me.

"Mr. Dabbs, what is it?" I asked. Egeria stopped fanning me with a napkin and looked over at him. Lara returned to her seat and her teacup. Festus, who had been demolishing several tartlets, paused mid-chew, and now all eyes were on Dabbs.

He bowed and then looked up at us. "When I was in Virginia tracing the Berilig and saw the search party looking for you, Eva, Shamus was there. He is the only one who could see me. The other humans were oblivious. I hid behind a tree and waited, barely securing my scent from the dogs, but they all pulled out of the woods except Shamus. He walked over to me, and we talked for a while. Once we made the quick connection that we were both acquainted with Bernadette and Eva, he informed me that Lady Bernadette succumbed . . ." He stopped talking.

"Succumbed? What do you mean by that, Mr. Dabbs?" I asked with a rising panic in my throat.

"She must have died, Eva," Lara said bluntly.

I was unable to make sense of what they were saying. It was Mr. Robinson who was sick and died, surely not Ms. B.! "What do you mean?" I pushed back at Dabbs, the bearer of bad news.

"Shamus was quite in a stew. The estate was already up in arms at your disappearance to the point they were taking steps to put you on a milk carton, whatever that means. Mr. Robinson was still in the hospital, recovering from pneumonia, when apparently, Lady Bernadette was found yesterday fallen over in the berry patch, must have had a heart attack or something." Mr. Dabbs was doing his best to relay the story as Shamus had revealed it.

I sat frozen, taking in all the news. I stood and instinctively walked to the front door. I needed fresh air. I needed the sun and the sky and the trees and the birds. I stepped through the front door into the open air and inhaled a deep breath of air, letting it out in an even deeper sigh. Kort appeared from around the side of the cottage.

"Everything OK, miss?"

"Yes, thank you." I said remotely.

He slunk back inconspicuously but still in my line of sight.

I became aware of all the extra clothing on me and began to remove the jacket, mesh vest, and belt with the dagger and sheath. Feeling lighter, I sat on the stoop and hugged my knees to my chest, trying to slow my breathing, feeling a kind of panic trying to overtake me.

Lara came out. "I brought you some medicinal tea. It will help calm and soothe you." She knelt beside me and offered a steaming clay mug with primitive designs etched on the sides. I accepted it gratefully.

Hours passed after that. I was eventually led to a bed and told to rest. The supposed death of Ms. Bernadette couldn't be true, I told myself. Could ANY of this be true? The part of me that held on to the fading slivers of logic and reality testing was numb. I was unable to think or feel anything further at this point.

I think I slept, wondering about the raid on the castle and if Shamus was able to capture Sinnott. Festus was dispatched quietly to spy on the battle and report back to us. Kort argued a bit about letting Festus out of his sight but was reminded I was his primary job. Kort remained outside, walking the perimeter of the cottage and keeping guard. Nemi arrived from the glade too, and between them, they could keep all of us under surveillance.

CHAPTER 23

F ESTUS KNEW THE secret trails and hidden paths better than anyone, and once again, he was trotting with a destination in mind. He stayed off the main road leading to the castle and decided to approach it from behind, through a wooded vale. As he drew nearer to where the castle was situated, he could hear some shouts and the strange sound of popping gunfire. He had slung around his neck an antiquated pair of binoculars, which he now focused on the action before him.

He saw the guardians and the hired army in a skirmish out front. Festus lifted his eyes to the top of the castle and spotted a few soldiers lining the parapet, releasing occasional arrows down into the fray. Festus moved a little closer, making sure he stayed very low, scooching forward on his belly. He decided to make a run forward, putting him closer to the castle, his eye fixed on a small door or postern gate leading to a cellar, most likely. Festus knew his small size would be easy to hide and conceal inside the castle, and he wanted to get an idea of what was happening to Sinnott, before bringing the news back to the council.

Fate was in his favor as he dove through the cellar door unscathed and unspotted. He brushed himself off and stood to his full height of four feet, letting his eyes adjust to the dark cellar room. He heard a moan coming from a corner and paused.

"Who goes there?" Festus whispered loudly.

"A friend of the queen" was the response. The voice was male and weary-sounding. Festus knew it instantly.

"Gunter!" he called out.

Festus reached the body of Gunter lying on his back.

"What, man? Where are you hit?" Festus whispered, still not sure if others were stashed away nearby.

"In my side here. I've lost a lot of blood." Festus was chagrinned, not having anything to help his friend. He could hardly lift or assist him either; Gunter was a full-size Druid, probably six feet tall.

"Let me see what I can find. Are there others down here with you? Do you know?"

"I don't think so. I haven't heard anyone."

Festus began exploring the cellar, looking for light and cloth or bandages. Anything. He fumbled with a candle and some matches, and the soft illumination helped immensely.

He located some cloths and a bowl for water, and soon, he was kneeling beside Gunter, attempting to clean up some blood to see the extent of the wound.

Gunter asked to drink the water first, saying he had been down in the cellar since yesterday. "How is everyone else?"

Festus filled him in slowly, especially in lieu of the deaths of Astrid and Bernadette and the arrival of Shamus. Gunter swore and complained because he couldn't do anything.

"Just try not to die, Gunter," Festus admonished. "We don't need any more of that."

After washing Gunter's wound and wrapping it in cloths, knowing it would need stitches, Festus agreed to spy on what was happening upstairs before getting more medical help for Gunter. He found dried meat of some kind and a bushel of apples, from which he supplied Gunter a small ration, before scurrying up the circular stone stairs. He found himself in the butler's pantry adjoining the keep of the castle and heard fighting coming from the great hall. He stayed hidden in a lower cupboard, and it was a good thing he did because soon, a couple of soldiers backed into the room, with guns aiming out into the castle keep.

"Who's shooting at us?" one soldier asked the other. "Those lousy guardians don't have guns!"

"Well it seems they do now! Simon went down! Nearly got me too!" the other soldier growled.

Their little conversation was interrupted by a frantic shout, followed by a barrage of yelling from fighters on a warpath, crying charge. Festus wished he knew who was charging who, so he just waited. The sounds of metal clashing swords and physical thrusts and punches and all the human grunts and cries that came along with fighting blared from the great room.

Then he detected a familiar guardian whistle, unique to the commander with various whistle sounds for various signals. And then he could hear many feet running and climbing the circular stone stairs to the second floor. The two hired guns to Sinnott's army taking cover in the pantry now plunged forward and fired shots at the running guardians. Festus winced as he heard someone go down.

With the battle moving upstairs, Festus ventured out of his hiding spot to see if he could help the fallen guardian. He was able to drag, with excessive huffing and puffing, the slain man back into the pantry. Festus could see a clean round hole in the man's shoulder with blood starting to pour out. The guardian was stunned, having never been hit by a bullet before, but he soon found he could get back up and keep going since the shot was in the shoulder.

"Stay behind, friend, and thanks for your help. If we have more wounded, I will send them to you."

"Send them to the cellar below. I've got one down there already." The guardian took off up the stairs.

Festus was torn between staying to see how the battle went or running back to the cottage for medical help. He decided to see if the guardians had any medics outside first.

He ventured to the main doors and saw the remains of a massacre. He was shocked, his eyes reeling from carnage. Fighters on both sides were strewn across the camp area set up by Sinnott's army. There was blood everywhere, and the abandoned swords, spears, guns, and arrows of the attack lay in the mess as small fires flickered or smoldered all around. Festus could feel the oppression of a heavy cloud that lingered after a species completed a great slaughter on itself.

Before he could move another muscle, a pack of guardians burst out of the woods carrying stretchers and bundles of medical aid. Each guardian was wearing a white cloth emblazoned with a red feather tied around their upper arm. Festus knew the symbol for the guardians was the feather and used in this way meant medical service. He ran up to one and offered his assistance.

They tended to the fallen guardians first as those with the most severe wounds were hoisted on the stretchers and carried back into the woods. Festus wondered where they were taken but stayed in the camp to help. A woman named Hestia was the apparent leader of the medical crew. She was moving from one injured person to the next and giving orders for their care. Festus started to follow her so that he could let her know about Gunter in the castle. But she was so busy he finally helped himself to some supplies and detoured from the camp, deciding to avoid the front doors of the castle since the battle was waging inside, and made his way back to Gunter.

As he found his way back down to the cellar, he could hear the sound of gunfire coming from upstairs. *I hope they got him,* Festus thought, *and end this whole mess.*

Gunter was resting on the floor, still weak. Festus drew a lamp nearby, and working with the nimble hands and fingers of a carpenter, he stitched up Gunter's side wound, packed it with herbal balm, and bandaged it up properly. He found in his supplies a vial of herbal tincture and poured it in Gunter's mouth, hoping it would help for pain and anti-infection. With Gunter resting more peacefully, Festus collected his medic supplies and went upstairs to see if others might need help.

CHAPTER 24

I WOKE UP FROM a hard nap, no dreams, no visions, nothing but a powerful sleep. It took a minute to get my bearings. I remembered I was in Lara's cottage. I had slept curled up in a smaller bed than I was used to, and there was a battle going on at the castle. With that thought, I leaped out of the bed and wandered into the kitchen for an update.

Everything was quiet; no one was around. I went to the back door and looked outside. No sign of Kort or Nemi or the council members. I went to the front door, and there, I found Nemi sitting on the stoop.

"Nemi! What's going on? Where is everyone?" The position of the sun and shadows led me to think it was late afternoon. I must have slept for hours then. Nemi jumped to attention.

"Kort escorted them to the castle. Sinnott was arrested and put in the dungeon. They were rounding up all his henchmen and trying to pay off the army to go back to their homes." A wave of profound relief swept through my body upon hearing about these developments - that justice was being swiftly served to Sinnott. "Well, that is good news!" I exclaimed. I then sat on the steps and invited him to return to his seat beside me imagining how tiresome being a guard and on your feet all the time must be. I felt deep admiration for the selfless and brave efforts of these mystical beings. He declined politely.

"I have been cleared to escort you to the castle when you woke, if you would like."

"Oh yes, let me get my stuff." I went in and dressed myself in the armor and boots. "Do I need all this?" I called out to Nemi.

He stood in the doorway to reply, "I think yes, to be safe, not sorry."

I concurred, and spying some tartlets still on the plate, I picked two for each of us. Nemi hesitated, and I said, "It's between us," and he seemed grateful for the snack.

We set out from the cottage and took the road to the castle. I wanted to chat with Nemi. He seemed like a nice kid, although he was probably close to my age. He was still socially awkward, as late teen boys can be, but he appeared well-trained as a guardian, although still low in rank. Out of respect for his job and training, I did not talk too much, ask personal questions, or try to glean more information from him, which allowed him to do his job well. He was impressively alert and vigilant. At one point, we were approached by several village men, anxious to know what was going on. I would have said more, but I let Nemi provide the details, which he did very minimally. The villagers trailed behind us a little longer until Nemi stopped, turned around, and respectfully asked them to stay back until the area was officially declared safe to civilians.

As we approached the castle yard, guardians were standing in a large circle, guarding the perimeter. I could see ahead to the battleground and the medics now running a makeshift aid station. The guards parted to let us through, but we were instructed not to enter the castle just yet. Nemi and I wandered through the makeshift clinic, and I was surprised to see the patients were not only guardians but also soldiers on Sinnott's team. Hired soldiers were packing up gear and setting off on foot, looking sullen and eager to get back home to various parts of the queendom, carrying their wages for an abbreviated job. I overheard some grumbling they thought this job was semi-permanent. Sinnott must have planned to keep them on indefinitely.

I found Hestia standing at a small folding table with medical and herbal supplies strewn in piles and sacks all around. A large cauldron of hot water was suspended from a metal tripod over a fire and simmering. Metal dishpans were filled with the simmering water and used to help wash the wounded and clean instruments. To my surprise, Hestia was talking on what looked like a military-grade walkie-talkie. Radio and communication technology had not reached this realm, and I couldn't imagine that it ever would. But clearly, it just had.

She saw me and beckoned me over. "Copy that," she said into the walkie-talkie. "Eva, you will be needed in the castle. Just wait here. Someone will come for you." Hestia saw me eyeing the walkie-talkie and looking at her. "Pretty cool, huh?" she said.

"Hestia, how do you know how to use this stuff? Where did you get it?" I felt caught off guard, and something started to nag at me. Her familiarity with modern technology and her use of a modern phrase just now seemed odd. A surge of adrenaline yanked at my heart, which started beating faster. *Did I miss something?* I thought. I glanced over at Nemi. He was nearby, keeping an eye on me, and I could tell he was giving the radio equipment a curious look.

Hestia smiled. "Don't worry, Eva, your friend Shamus is a friend of mine too. Long story. Later." And with that, she went off to help a patient. Shamus and Hestia? Yes, that needed illumination, but I knew I wouldn't find out just yet.

Wishing there was something I could help with, I scanned behind the aid station near the woods and saw another firepit had been started, and a small crew was cooking food, some kind of stew. There was an opening in the woods where guardians and medics were traversing in and out, and I assumed there was a door to the underground caves nearby. Over by the castle entrance, guardians were lighting fire to several torches on poles and placing them strategically near the entrance and along the front walls. The sun was much lower in the sky by now and would set behind the castle, spreading early shadows on this side. Additional torches were going up around the aid station. A bowl of stew was brought to me with a cup of red wine. Nemi was also fed, for which I was glad.

I watched as a group of about a dozen villagers, escorted by guardians, passed through the encampment and were led into the castle. I imagined they must be part of the transition process, gathering to determine the next steps in the government platform for this innocent, charming town of Demistrath. I noticed I rarely thought of my life in Virginia anymore, but that was understandable, I guess. I felt a little guilty because those were my people after all, and my family, they loved me, I knew, and must be going through a painful time thinking I was kidnapped, which was the significance of the search party and the photo on the milk jugs that poor Mr. Dabbs was trying to make sense of in his race back to Virginia to get help. I took a deep breath and looked up at the dusky indigo sky, clear of clouds and with twinkling stars starting to dot the deep blue canvas above. I called out to Ms. Bernadette and opened my mind to her. There was a silence in response and only the gently dancing stars overhead and a rising half-moon.

"Such a beautiful world, isn't it?" a deep tenor voice said from behind me. I didn't have to turn around to know it was Lurien. Where had they come from? I did not see them emerge from the castle. I could feel Lurien standing quietly at my side now, gazing up at the sky with me. "I have heard it said your people have flown to the moon and back. Even set foot on the moon. That is incomprehensible to us."

I turned and looked at Lurien's profile, so perfect in symmetry and with a straight angle of nose and firm chin and jawline. Lurien turned to make contact with my face. I could feel warm, dry fingers reach for mine and gently entwine with mine in a caress of such tenderness; the simplicity of the gesture was staggering. I was thoughtless and speechless.

"My lady, if I may, you are required in the castle for a meeting of the village council, the Elemental Council, and the guardians. I am here to escort you."

A brush of anticipation mixed with fear nuzzled through my heart and belly. *Something's up,* I thought. Once again, I was being pulled into a new chapter of Demistrath written by an unknown author, and here I was, walking into a new page. I waited to follow

Lurien, but instead, the commander gestured for me to walk first and then fell into step just slightly behind me. I could feel a hand on the small of my back guiding me as we walked toward the castle doors, anyone remotely nearby pausing to let us pass in a distinctly respectful bow to the commander. I felt rather like second fiddle to a celebrity; Lurien was still outfitted in fighting uniform, a top military commander.

Guards opened the castle doors as we approached, with a fisted salute over their hearts. We crossed into the castle keep and into the great hall. I almost expected the black cat to show up as she was here the last time I walked across this floor of flagstones. Up ahead, a meeting had gathered around the great table, and people were taking chairs and places on benches, some as deep as three rows out. I could feel Lurien's hand give my waist an encouraging brush before letting go, gesturing me to an open space near the head of the table. Lurien stepped into the head spot. I looked around the table and recognized many who had assembled. My buddies from the cottage sat in a row at the table. Shamus was not far from me, across the table. Our eyes met, and I kept my face devoid of expression to match his stoic countenance. I was still not sure what was going on and didn't want to let my guard down. Lurien's advisor opened the meeting with a summary of the takeover that ousted Dev Sinnott, who was now under lock and key in the dungeon. His bodyguards and confidants were also arrested and jailed. No lives were lost, to everyone's relief. I wondered how Shamus and the guardians had managed to overpower Sinnott, but those details were not revealed at this meeting.

The questions at hand were the future of Dev Sinnott and his sentencing and those of his party, and to identify the next ruler of Demistrath. The councils were here to vote for these measures. A spokesperson from both the village council and the Elemental council would be then tasked with casting the votes of their governing bodies. The advisor continued to speak. "The articles of governance will need new amendments to entail the next queen or monarch. We cannot afford to leave the gates open anymore to infiltrators, such as Sinnott, regardless of their lineage, without the sanction of the electorate."

A village councilman spoke up. "But we have always relied on the ruling queen to identify and install the next queen. Why did that not happen with Queen Merideth?"

A murmur broke out in the assembled group, and some side conversations started up. The advisor let out a sharp whistle, which effectively silenced the room.

"My friends, we must keep order."

Just then, I felt something soft brush against my leg. I shifted my leg and bumped up against it, pushing it away with my foot. Then to my horror, it began climbing my leg and under my tunic. By now, I was simultaneously jerking up out of my seat and, with my hands, trying to brush this creature away. I stifled a scream as I saw a flash of black fur dart off my lap and under the table. I had just caused a commotion and attracted the annoyed, baffled, and surprised stares of the collective surrounding the table.

I shook my head and remained standing. "I offer my apology. I believe I was just assaulted by a black cat!"

Mr. Dabbs stood. "Stop that cat, somebody!" But it was too late. No one seemed to know Anastasia like I did. She would be perched far away grooming herself, making it hard to believe my story. A couple of guardians were pacing the room and table, looking for the feline, but she had vanished.

"What is this distraction, and can we trust a human to behave long enough?" The same village councilman was now standing and pointing at me. "I, for one, am not comfortable with the presence of these outsiders in our inner sanctum meeting." He was not alone in his thoughts. I caught a few sympathetic mutterings.

"If it pleases the council, I will dismiss myself. However, I was summonsed to this meeting and mean no harm. I am familiar with that cat. She belonged with Sinnott. Mr. Dabbs is right, she should be apprehended as soon as possible." I sat and then realized the meeting had quieted down, and everyone was listening to me. I turned to Lurien, who nodded.

"Eva is correct, she is not at this meeting on her own accord. The guardians brought her here, after her rescue from the castle. She was abducted in Virginia by Sinnott's cat and taken prisoner, for what purpose, we are still piecing together. It is important, my friends, that we remain open minded in this ordeal. Demistrath is out of balance and tilted on its axis from the recent events. In the absence of a sitting queen, the guardians are to maintain order and protocol. We suffered another loss with our village sage, Astrid, in this takeover. Normally, the Elemental Council would name the queen's successor, but we will have to divert to new protocols established by the larger council sitting here in this room. It is essential that we listen to each other and make a decision, which some will not like, but others will, and we will go with a majority vote."

Lurien continued. "It is imperative we identify and install the next monarch as soon as possible and have the coronation for Demistrath. Word has reached the other villages of the queendom that we were under seize. The mood of the land is tense. We have sent for the oracle and be advised all of us must remain here at the castle until we get this done. Food and bed will be provided, and if you must send word to your families, any of you, messengers will be dispatched."

As can be expected, the council launched into a splintered band of side conversations, talking among themselves. I was vaguely still concerned about the cat, who had breached my space yet again. Murderous thoughts shot through my head, and I could feel the heat of anger rising. I wanted her captured. She was a menace to me from the very beginning.

The meeting seemed to be on a break as council members relayed communication to the designated messengers. Lurien had turned to consult with the advisors. I looked around the room; there must have been about twenty or so, including my friends of the Elemental Council, who would be sequestered in the castle to select the next queen. I found my way over to Mr. Dabbs, Festus, Lara, and Egeria. They were discussing the status of the wounded Gunter. He had been treated and was resting in a room upstairs with a few other patients. Shamus joined our little circle.

"So what's next in this enchanting little kingdom of yours?" he said.

"It's a queendom, Shamus," I replied, knowing my friends would be too polite to correct him. "So how did you all bring Sinnott down?"

"We used the old-fashioned element of surprise and distraction. While they were busy dealing with the distraction, we were able to enter the office and disarm Sinnott and his guards. Then the guardians swooped in from all sides. The bloke had to surrender. I think the hired army was getting a little suspect of their boss, and the guardians ultimately prevailed, shall we say? And to be sure, the guardians are an impressively trained lot, well-coordinated, and highly attuned. Their leader"—and here, Shamus turned and gestured over to Lurien—"is amazingly calm. They read every signal. They are silent and stealthy. It's like watching a choreographed ballet. I'm impressed."

An advisor approached our little group and informed us we would be part of the team meeting with the oracle, that we were to stand by. I noticed a buffet of food and drink was being set up on a sideboard near the table, and some folks were starting to help themselves. Shamus excused himself for the food, and the rest of us followed. I welcomed another moment to relax a little.

"Who or what is this oracle?" I asked my friends.

Lara spoke up. "A seer, a knower. Some call her a witch. She is very old, and strange, and reclusive. The queens of Demistrath have consulted her and the oracles before her for a long time. Especially when wisdom is needed regarding outsiders or outside forces. It's been a while since our queen would have called on the oracle."

"Sinnott had his own oracle. It was a machine. Do you all know anything about that? It's probably still upstairs in his office. Apparently, he used it to locate me when he sent his cat to Virginia."

My question was left hanging. Our party became distracted from one another by food and other passing conversations, so I sat beside Shamus to talk with him privately. There was so much I wanted to know about his entry into this story, his connection to Hestia, and how much he really knew about Demistrath.

We had barely started into the conversation when a wave of distraction filtered into the great hall from the direction of the cellar stairs. The oracle had arrived, and heads were craning to see where the commotion was coming from. A team of guardians tried to form protective positions around her, but as her feet stepped onto the floor from the cellar, she pushed her way among them and stood searching the corner of the great hall, where our council was mingling. She was a curious sight, standing about five feet tall, dressed in layers of skirts and tunic blouses, her shoulders wrapped in a muslin cape, the pointy toed shoes on her feet were adorned in stones, a twisted branch of a walking stick gripped in an arthritic hand, and cloth medicine bag slung across her body, hanging at her side. Her face was broad and round, and her hair was strands of calico shades: brown, black, white, blond, and orange. There was no way to guess her age, but it was her eyes, in the end, that grabbed my attention as they quickly found mine, and she paused to stare me down. Soon, the room noticed she had singled me out and began glancing back and forth between us.

"Take me to the chamber," the oracle blurted out as her eyes lingered a while longer before she turned away. Lurien nodded to the guards, and they guided her up the stairs. I had been unable and unwilling to turn away from her gaze, and now I reached behind me to take a seat on the bench. *Not again,* I thought as I tried to collect myself from her cryptic attention. I was really starting to wish for my ordinary life and wondering why I was continually culled from the crowd and singled out. Lara and Shamus checked in with me, and Lara muttered what I was thinking. "That was weird. Maybe she doesn't like humans."

"I wish I knew what was going on," I replied.

"Right," Shamus said and stood, walking away, to bring us more information, I hoped. Lara kindly stayed seated with me, and this small gesture soothed me slightly. The larger council kept their distance. I didn't blame them. This whole experience was feeling shaky and insecure. So much of the confidence I had started out with was ebbing away, and what started as a curious adventure with Ms. B. now seemed like a runaway train. I sure missed Ms. B. Tears began to run down my cheeks, and I fought hard not to burst into weeping. Lara put an arm around my shoulders, and I leaned into her. I somehow managed to cry quietly, my body heaving in silent gasps. She handed me a cloth for my nose. I hoped no one was noticing. I thought of Ms. B. dying in the garden. I prayed she had not suffered. I recalled her communications with me since her death and realized she was OK wherever she was. My thoughts went to Mr. Robinson, lying in a hospital now a widow. I wondered what story Shamus had used to stay away from the household. I thought of Betsy probably worried sick about me. For the first time, my life back home started to grab ahold of my heart. My mother and brothers and sisters surely wondered where I was. Ferncliff Estate dealing with a funeral on top of my disappearance. I realized it was time for me to return home. After all, Virginia, not Demistrath, was where I belonged.

I wiped my face and pulled myself together. Lara looked relieved. "There you go, Ms. Eva. That's a girl." Folks here would never know or fully understand my other life in Virginia, and my people in Virginia would never understand, much less believe, this whole other world to which I was now a key player. I guess Mr. Dabbs was right. I was a Polaris, a connector between worlds, able to travel, communicate, connect, and weave between them. It seemed my abilities were stronger here in Demistrath. But then I was getting hits of intuition back in Virginia; I remembered the déjà vus of Ms. B. and me in a castle, the dream back in time to Roser Park in Florida and seeing Bernadette's parents, and hearing Mr. Dabbs call from the woods. I was tuning in there too. I guess it was just my time to awaken to this part of me.

I sucked in a deep breath and placed both my feet on the floor. I stood, adjusted my clothing, straightened my belt, and smoothed my hair. Lurien was walking toward us in commander form, so I waited at attention. I caught a fleeting spark in those eyes as they briefly met mine. For a moment, my heart calmed, and I remained poised while suppressing the urge to grab Lurien's hands.

"It is time to go meet the oracle," Lurien said, and I crossed the great hall with the other selected ones.

CHAPTER 25

T HE SECOND FLOOR of the castle was a series of rooms that flanked both sides of a wide, spacious hallway. I was relieved when we were led past Sinnott's office, which I never wanted to see again, and farther down to "the chamber" as the oracle called it. In addition to Lurien and one advisor, our group included Shamus and me, the four members of the Elemental Council, and several guards, including Kort and Nemi. We were brought in through an arched doorway and led around a corner and up a wide expanse of stone stairs and into a round room. The light of dusk streamed in through an opening to air and sky above that left a circle of pale light in the center of the floor, the rest of the room under roof and darkness. Wall-mounted fire torches burned around the perimeter walls. A round stone table standing on a pedestal of stone occupied the center of the circle of light. There were ritual objects on the table, and a single tall purple column candle was burning briskly, fanned by the snippets of breezes that made it all the way down from the skylight opening. I was suddenly reminded of the Warm Springs bathhouse. The way light poured down was similar.

As we assembled to one side of the table, the oracle stepped out of a darkness and approached the altar. She motioned to Lara to come forward. Lara's face was full of fear and caution, but she stepped close to the table. The oracle did not speak out loud but guided Lara with gestures. We all watched with rapt fascination. My heart went out to Lara, who had to shoulder the burden of being the first. The oracle pricked one of Lara's fingers with the point of a dagger and squeezed a few drops of blood onto a plate. She then swirled the drops of blood with droplets of water and sprinkles of what looked like ash, taken from containers on the altar. With a long matchstick, the oracle lit one end from the purple candle and then held the flame to the mixture on the plate. The briefest of flickers ignited but then nothing. The oracle made a swishing sound while exhaling. She motioned Lara to step back and called for a helper in the shadows, who ran forth with a bucket of water, in which she rinsed the plate and dried it with an altar cloth, followed by a burning bundle of sage to smudge the plate. She pointed to Egeria next. The very same ritual was executed with Egeria. Again, nothing caught on fire from the blood and ash mixture. I knew my turn was next and started to step forward, but the oracle stopped me with a hand signal. Mr. Dabbs and Festus were both given the ritual treatment instead.

The oracle was clearly trying to be as methodical as possible in this discerning ritual for the next monarch and apparently was extending it to all Elemental Council members. Even Shamus and Lurien were tested. By now, I was beginning to fade in my fascination as the ritual was starting to feel a little hokey to me. After yet another plate rinse and dry, it was my turn. The oracle stared at me with almost a sinister intensity, so I kept my brave face on and returned her gaze. She was squeezing droplets of blood from my middle finger. Then the water and the ash were added. Next, the flame was held to the mixture. I was about to look away but was pulled back by a dancing little blue flame flickering over my blood. The oracle became completely still as she watched the flame, and my friends grew quiet as they leaned in to catch a glimpse of the flame. Someone in the group whispered, "Is it her?"

The oracle looked up at me and gestured for my hand. She grabbed my hand in her gnarly clutch and opened my palm to stare at the lines mapped out there. A guttural groan of recognition sounded from her throat.

"You!" she said to me and started to walk away, turning to gesture for me to follow. I was hesitant to leave my group and turned to look at Mr. Dabbs and Lurien standing to my left. Mr. Dabbs had a pensive expression on his face that was not surprised. Lurien's face registered nothing in particular.

"It's OK, you can follow her. I'll be close by."

I glanced at the others, reluctant to leave their familiar and safe company. Kort stepped forward, but Lurien held him back.

"I've got this one. Stay with the others."

I was grateful for Lurien's protection. I reached for their hand and felt the warm, comforting grasp in return as we followed the oracle through a low, narrow door both of us had to lower our heads as we passed through and emerged into what must have been her lair, or study, or lab, whatever the term would be for where mystical and magical practice is conducted by such folk. The oracle removed her cape and hood and draped it over a rocking chair. She lit a few candles and added some dried herbs into a simmering cauldron bubbling with a wine-colored brew. She ladled the brew into two wooden goblets and handed them to Lurien and me.

"Drink. It is time. You, Eva of Virginia, you are the next queen of Demistrath and the queendom of Terragon. You, protector and guardian Lurien, you are her personal right hand and consort. "It is your destiny. There is no refusing this." The room was silent. I started to tremble. I could feel my gut twisting into knots. A small part of me had seen this coming – as soon as the oracle demanded that I follow her – but my body was rebelling against this new information. I felt my stomach lurching with the uncertainty and intense doubt over this verdict. "How - how can this be?" I stuttered, looking between her and Lurien. "I don't -"

The oracle closed her eyes and began to elaborate in a staccato voice. "Your becoming queen has been anticipated and foretold by fourth dimension seers and oracles for a century or more. It coincides with a major shift on the planet taking place in the next millennium, counting down in a span of 25 to 50 years to bring in the next 5000 year earth cycle, or age. This major shift is to lead the planet out of war, poverty, greed, corruption, and disease. False structures of separation, us and them, will collapse. You, child, are part of that unifying process." With that, the Oracle sat down on the rocking chair and promptly fell asleep.

I felt utterly overwhelmed. Prior to my ceremony with the oracle, I had resolved to return to Virginia. The image of my mother, sisters, and brothers flooded my mind. What would they think? When could I see them? How could I see them? A searing pang of sorrow struck my heart at the thought of worrying them, of losing them. My stomach continued to turn over, the physical pain increasing.

What did being a queen of a foreign world even mean? What would be expected of me? My mind drifted to my life as a staff member at Ferncliff Estate. If I accept this new fate, I might never step foot there again. How would my dear friend Betsy and the others fare now that Ms. B had passed on? Would they be ok? Betsy would be distraught that I left her so abruptly, with no goodbye. My body shivered with uneasiness as these worried thoughts raced through my mind.

At that moment, Lurien reached for my hand. "What is it, Eva? I'm here. Tell me what you are thinking." I looked to see Lurien staring intently at me with a gentle but concerned expression on their face, since I had still not spoken a word in response. A slight snore was coming from the rocking chair, the Oracle seemed so unconcerned about her pronouncement she fell asleep. I felt a palpable connection between Lurien and myself in the otherwise silent inner sanctum of the Oracle. In that instant, I felt my clenched stomach slowly release its tension, like it was exhaling a long, deep breath. A gentle warmth started to spread through my body. Ms. Bernadette had told me to go on, to embrace my experience in Demistrath. And despite the risk and uncertainty, I could sense that somehow, someway, I would be able to keep my family and friends in my life, even if at a distance. The tension and worry had dissipated quicker than it had arrived. It would not be the same. But this wasn't a forever goodbye.

I squeezed their hand tightly with mine. "I don't know what will happen to the realm where I'm from, Lurien." I spoke quietly.

I could see Lurien's expression become more pained. I could tell they were trying to remain neutral, but that there was an inner wave of emotion also sweeping through them.

"But" I continued, "it will have to carry on without me. Apparently, I am to be Queen." A rush of joy and relief burst open on Lurien's face. It was time for a new chapter. I was needed here in Demistrath. And Lurien would be here to protect me.

Lurien made an elegant salute to me and we smiled at each other. It was then we realized we were both still holding our cups, so we clinked glasses and took a sip. It tasted like an earthy wine; I could detect sassafras and cedar. We set our cups down on the table, and Lurien bowed slightly to the sleeping oracle, and I followed suit, and we turned to step out of the lair and back into the round chamber.

Our friends swarmed toward us.

"What happened? What did she say?"

"She named me the next queen of Demistrath, and Lurien, Commander Lurien, is to be my right hand and . . ." I heard myself drift off.

"Consort," Lurien finished for me.

Shamus spoke first and broke the ice. "Well, I'll be damned, lassie. Or should I call you Your Royal Highness? And Commander Consort, charmed, I'm sure!"

Shamus was having too much fun with this, and I could tell the council was awkwardly keeping quiet as he winked at Lurien.

Kort and Nemi had flanked me again, and I said to the waiting group, "Let's go back to the cottage. We have a lot of planning to do."

CHAPTER 26

L ARA'S SWEET LITTLE cottage calmed me a bit. Warm, cozy, and welcoming, I felt safe and secure here. The five remaining members of the council plus myself and Shamus crammed into the kitchen. Missing were Astrid and Gunter. Lara was obviously relieved to be in her kitchen. She was clanking kettles and cups, preparing some tea. I watched her adding pinches of herbs into the teapot, blending her own mixture, which I was sure would be soothing and clarifying. She intuitively knew what was needed to aid the health of us all. Egeria was laying out the council *Grimoire*, the book of shadows or book of magic and instruction, from which she seemed so versed in finding information and interpreting it for the Elemental Council and Demistrath. Shamus was hovering near Lara, trying to snitch some scones, and it dawned on me there was a little flirtatious energy going on between them. I glanced over at Lurien, who had returned to their corner as I had seen them the first time. Lurien sat on the stool and picked the whittling knife and held a stump of wood in the other hand but did not proceed to carve, only looking up at me with what seemed a look of uncertainty. I had not seen that expression ever on Lurien's face before. I gave my most encouraging smile to Lurien. I was trying to recall what a consort did exactly. The word seemed Old Testament biblical, for some reason. King David and his consorts. I don't know. Maybe I was just making that up.

The conversation that ensued around the table was brisk and lively. Mr. Dabbs and Egeria were particularly engrossed in understanding Demistrathian protocol for the coronation and installation of a new queen. The public would have to meet me first. Queen Merideth had ruled for four decades, so some around the table vaguely remembered her coronation. Festus was helpful in recalling past coronations, usually three-day affairs, where the festivities start and end at the castle, but the entire village's civil and commercial operations would go on pause as citizens from across the queendom would arrive to enjoy the party. From what I could tell, the whole village turned into a grand bed-and-breakfast, providing lodging and food to the visitors, who, in turn, shared the cost through barter or services. I was starting to feel some excitement listening to the planning and descriptions until I remembered I would be front and center to this fanfare, and suddenly, my nerves quickened.

Shamus had found Gunter's stored liquor bottle and was becoming rather jolly. I had never seen him "off duty" like this, and he was one of those people who didn't seem to worry and could openheartedly enjoy the moment while imbibing in alcohol. Even though I did not drink (before coming to Demistrath), I had plenty of opportunity to observe those who did and learned there were several categories of inebriation people would display: the mean ones, the happy ones, the sad and forlorn ones, and those who just fell asleep. I would probably be the latter.

It was nighttime now, and I was feeling the effects of what seemed like the longest day. I realized others were weary too, so I suggested we tuck in for the night and resume tomorrow. Lara offered me a bed, but I begged Lurien to take me back to my room at the glade. To me, that felt like the bed I wanted to sleep in tonight. Plus, something was urging me to see Dawn again. Lurien wanted to object, but Kort and Nemi seemed eager to get back too, so the four us collected our armor and battle gear and made one more exerted effort to heave these bodies on a hike "home." Nemi led the way carrying a lantern, Kort next, followed by me, and Lurien took the rear. I had no idea how or where the rest would sleep tonight, but that was not my problem to fix, thank the goddess.

Lurien personally escorted me all the way to my room to make sure I was safely installed. Two new guards were already planted outside the door, relieving Kort and Nemi. I turned to face Lurien standing in my open door and was suddenly overwhelmed with desire to pull my consort into the room with me. Instantly, the meaning of the word landed like an epiphany in my mind. Lurien could see my desire, and I was quite certain felt it too. We stood in an awkward pause before I started to reach out, but Lurien put up a hand in front of their heart and mouthed the words "Not now," making eye glances in the direction of the guards.

Then Lurien said out loud for the benefit of any nearby listening ears or eyes, "Sleep well, tonight, my lady. Until the morning then," and gave me the most charming wink I had ever received. It had a magical effect on me, and I fell asleep the moment my head touched the pillow.

CHAPTER 27

T HE NEXT TWO weeks became a bustling whirlwind of village-wide activity. The castle, first of all, had to be deeply cleaned and scrubbed and aired out. Gunter and the other patients were moved to a convalescent home, although Gunter defied orders and removed himself early and was found walking around to observe the activity or lounging at Lara's cottage but, most of all, presiding over the village council meetings. Turned out the metalsmith position on the Elemental Council served as the moderator of the larger governing council. I was introduced to all the important people in Demistrath and instructed daily one on one by various persons educating me on the civic and royal workings and duties of this queendom. The notebook and pen I brought from Virginia became essential as I took copious notes, a method of learning that had always worked best for me. But it really helped remember names and titles and essential duties.

I was measured for a new wardrobe and dressed every day by Dawn, who also developed the most creative hairstyles I had ever seen on myself or anyone else with my kind of hair. Like most royalty, I assume, there were various sashes, brooches, crowns, and jewelry that had certain assignments for when to be worn. But unlike the British monarch Queen Elizabeth, my version of these articles was much more rustic, to my pleasure, and I was delighted how this realm was interwoven with nature at every level. *Woodland adornment is so beautiful,* I thought, and in all this tizzy of activity, I started to enjoy daily walks outside, often with Dawn, and always escorted unobtrusively by my guards. The weather was turning to fall, the air was cooling down, and the sky was bluer than I could ever imagine. I wanted to reach out and hug the world on days like these. I was reminded of the opening scene in the movie *The Sound of Music,* where Maria, the main character, is singing on a hilltop in Austria, turning in circles with her arms stretched out wide. It was that kind of experience here.

Shamus, it was decided, would return to Virginia, with Mr. Dabbs's help and attend the funeral of Ms. B. Then he would put in his resignation to Ferncliff Estate and pretend to return to Scotland. But really, he would travel back to Demistrath and become, like myself, a missing person in our countries of birth. He and I had several opportunities to talk privately after the meeting with the oracle. It turned out Shamus contained inside his droll and rather stern demeanor a poet and a philosopher. He let his inner Scotsman come out much more in this realm, and he confided in me that he had few relationships in the human world to hold him there. He had always been nomadic and married to his work. An injury overseas while on an assignment forced him to retire as a journalist earlier than he preferred, and remembering Ms. Bernadette and fancying himself an adventure in America, he ended up as the chef of Ferncliff. With my encouragement, Shamus put in a bid with the council for approval to serve on the royal cabinet or inner circle. I could tell he was well versed in politics and people and someone who would be a great benefit to me. Having one other person from the human world to council me was a comfort. It also appeared he and Lara were developing a liking to each other, and they seemed well matched. I wanted to help that along. The Elemental Council seemed agreeable to bringing Shamus in, and they would have influence with the larger council.

Meanwhile, there was the issue of what to do with our prisoners. In addition to Sinnott, there were six others arrested in the rescue of the castle and still held in the dungeon cells. We made sure they were treated humanely, but we couldn't keep them forever. The village judge agreed to set up a criminal court to formally charge the prisoners with crimes of treason, and they would be sentenced to banishment from the queendom. The council expressed concern that Sinnott was cunning enough to continue to cause trouble or make his way back with reinforcements, even though the guardians would be patrolling with a heightened presence, especially in lieu of my installation as queen. Egeria came up with the idea to use the Berilig stone as a tracker and implant it into Sinnott's body so that his whereabouts would always be known. Shamus and I were quite amused at Egeria's modern sensibilities, and it was arranged that Lara and Egeria would undertake the surgery, after rendering Sinnott unconscious with a powerful set of herbs, and he would not know in the slightest he was tagged.

I learned there were still some rumblings in the village about a human sitting on the throne, and I myself was struggled with my new title, and certain I had no idea the extent of ramifications that awaited me. I saw Lurien often now but rarely alone. There was plenty of queendom business to take care of, and we fell into a working partnership that brought me joy and confidence. Lurien was probably one of the best people I knew; Betsy was another. The kind of person who is trustworthy, honest, capable, easygoing, and lives to their own impeccable standard without judging others who don't. I was grateful to my mother and my training at Ferncliff more and more each day when I found learning my new job as a queen was made easier by these earlier trainings in formality and comportment.

The night before my coronation, an uncanny opening occurred in the busy schedule where I was outside at the glade, enjoying an evening fire with a bunch of guardians and Dawn. We were drinking warm beverages, and Lurien was maintaining a beautiful fire in the pit. Quiet, jovial banter was exchanged. I was so smitten with the perfection of the experience and was deep in my five senses that I was barely aware the circle of friends began slowly getting smaller and smaller. My heart was overflowing with a love for everyone and everything. Lurien had come to sit beside me on the same log bench, our shoulders leaning into each other, our thighs touching. We sat in silence like this together for what seemed like a long time, watching the fire. Occasionally, Lurien would reach forward to shift the logs or add another one. I was faintly aware of Dawn's soft voice saying good night as she left the circle, and it was then I noticed Lurien and I were the only ones left. I felt Lurien stir, and I reached for their hand and spontaneously moved it up to my face, feeling the caress against my cheek.

"Eva," Lurien said, "tomorrow you will become my queen. There is something I want you to know."

I turned to face Lurien. The orange firelight illuminated the whole half of their face, creating a half-moon glow. Our faces were close, and I could see every plane of Lurien's jawline, cheekbones, nose, and forehead.

I gently touched their cheek, and our eyes were gazing deeply into each other. Lurien spoke again, softly, with a poignant pull on the words.

"I think it goes without saying, but I want to be sure. I have not loved another person romantically in a long time. I took the oath of guardian twelve years ago when I was eighteen. I was promoted to this position that I hold now, and it comes with vast responsibilities and commitment. Until I met you, I was not drawn to another in a way that ever interfered with my work. But now there are times, Eva, when I am not myself, I am distracted, and, and . . ." Here Lurien's voice faltered, and they looked away from me, a pained expression passing across the slate of that beautiful face.

"Ssshhhh," I said. "I will not come between you and your work, Lurien. And I have my work too. We must support each other."

"We will. But, Eva, how do you feel about me? I want to know."

"Oh, Lurien! Can't you tell? I am in so much love with you I can't think sometimes!" By now, Lurien was pulling me closer. I pressed a hand to Lurien's chest and leaned my face against their shoulder. "We have time" I said. "I want to know you longer." It sounded so corny to me, that I pulled up to look at Lurien's face.

Before I could say another word, Lurien grabbed my face in both hands and pressed their lips to mine, gently tasting each other for the first time. It was soft and searching, and we became deeply fastened together. I moved my hands to Lurien's waist and stomach and felt the strong muscles, and one hand brushed up Lurien's chest, feeling nothing but muscle and curves and soft but firm physical form.

My warrior, I thought. *My protector. My consort.*

Lurien left my lips and nuzzled my temples and into my hair and down my neck. I heard a tender moan.

Just when I thought I might lose control, Lurien pulled back and met my eyes again.

"You, dear woman, are delicious!"

I started to giggle, and then Lurien joined in, running their hands down my shoulders, arms, thighs. A playfulness took over, and we pulled each other off the bench and rolled onto the cool earth, lying by the fire; I could feel the heat from the embers and our aching yearning limbs, now entwined.

"It's too bad we missed Beltane. Then we could have loved on each other with no limits, interference, or consequence."

"Beltane?" I hoped people here wouldn't get tired of my endless questions about their everyday life.

"May 1. One of the eight Sabbats. The spring explosion of new life, fertility, you know."

I cuddled against Lurien's splendid body, feeling their long lean limbs and torso with my legs and arms. I wanted this night to go on forever. We kissed some more. Who knew kissing could be so interesting and ongoing and not a bit boring? Our hands moved around more freely over each other and then stopped for air and quiet stillness. We rolled on our backs and looked up at the distant sky, where stars cascaded in a spangled array, and the moon was in a waxing phase toward complete fullness. The oracle had given us the exact day for the coronation, saying it must happen on the next full moon, the harvest moon, in September. Tomorrow. Or was it already tomorrow? The fire was dying out. And we both instinctively collected ourselves, knowing it was time to end this beautiful moment. There would be more. Lurien rose in a single move to full standing and then held out a hand to me and lifted me to my feet from our little love nest.

"Come, Queen Eva of Demistrath, let's get you to bed."

CHAPTER 28

W HEN I AWOKE in the morning, my last night in my little sanctuary of a room underground in the glade, I was informed by Dawn it was raining.

"But it will pass, and the day will be beautiful," she said, "for you can be sure there are many using witchcraft in their morning rituals today to make it perfect."

"Are there many who practice the craft here in Demistrath? And are they called witches?"

"Just like in your world, the word 'witch' is not typically a welcomed word. People who tune into the sixth and seventh senses, who align themselves with the flow of the cosmic energy, who KNOW the oneness of all things and flow with that current, these are the ones called witches. In our realm, like in yours, many suffered and died because of these gifts, and for survival, the practice of witchcraft was deeply subverted to the point witches themselves chaffed at associating with the name. I can't think of any other word so violently abhorred and misunderstood. But yes, we have many here in Demistrath who believe in their own gifts and practice quietly. The word 'witch' itself comes from the old root word wit, meaning wisdom, knowledge. Women, sadly, often found their way into this craft because of their natural expression of empathy and emotion. But there are just as many men who have the wit and practice without knowing. Many animals practice it too."

I was so enthralled in this conversation. "But couldn't it be said that there are in every religion and every nation all over the world ones who practice witchcraft, but it goes by other names? Prayer, miracles, spirit, faith, prophesy, even the oracle?"

"It is all the same source."

"Then how can some people be so good and kind and some so evil?"

"They tap into different energies. It is like there are many roads running through the cosmos, and sometimes we travel a road we've chosen on purpose, and other times, we wander and get lost and find ourselves on roads that are unsafe, dangerous, treacherous. Sometimes we stay lost for a lifetime, or several lifetimes, until we can find our way to our course again, the road we were searching for."

"Oh, Dawn, I want to know all about this. Will you be my teacher?"

She paused in her movements, helping me bathe and dress.

"My queen, it would be my great honor," and with that, she gave a sweet little curtsy and a giggle.

I was festooned in a new gown of ivory and satin, and my hair worked into an updo that would allow for the crown to rest securely. I was adorned in necklaces and bracelets and felted ivory shoes with satin ribbing placed on my feet. I would have a cape and carry a scepter. All these final touches took place in the chamber room, with a crackling fire and many attendants moving around, talking among themselves with excitement. Hestia entered to offer her admiration and a cup filled with sparkling water, citrus, and ginger.

"Drink this. It will soothe your stomach. She dabbed some aromatic oil on my temples, neck, and wrists.

"It will keep you calm," she whispered. Then she briefly curtsied and moved away.

I felt like I was somewhat informed on what was happening today. I would be transported from the glade in an entourage of horses and carriages and brought to the castle for some opening ceremony. From there, the parade would travel from the castle to the village and arrive at the market plaza, by the river, where I was told the plaza had been transformed into a magical spectacle for the festivities. Citizens from all over the queendom of Terragon would be joining the Demistrathians in a banquet with music, merriment, and dance. The coronation was falling on a full moon and the Fall Equinox, making it a powerful time for new beginnings and fulfillment of hard work. My introduction to the people earlier in the past two weeks had gone well. The Elemental Council spent more time with the oracle to confirm my selection and appointment. For some reason, the Demistrathians gave credence to my appointment and accepted the blessing of the oracle and the Elemental Council. I thought they were also just relieved to have a new queen, a really good party, and then go back to their simple, happy routines. Frankly, that sounded really nice to me too.

I was not sure what I envisioned for my reigning years. I saw myself advancing my study and learning of all things fourth dimension and of the history of this queendom. I saw myself reconvening with my brothers and sisters in my realm – a realm that felt so distant now. I saw myself traveling and making state visits to other parts of the realm. I saw a reign of spiritual and creative growth, a society that felt love more than fear, and could enjoy the physical experience of being alive on this planet. In short, my reign would not only be about a focused time of healing and restoring balance, but also readiness for new commitments and elevating consciousness to a worldwide view and not just a provincial one.

As my royal carriage paraded slowly toward Demistrath, the sides of the road were lined with all manner of folk and animal, birds, and butterflies. Seriously. I was not making this up. They were cheering, singing, waving tree branches, and wearing garlands of flowers, and merry strains of music by harp, flute, drums, and tambourines speckled the air. As foretold, the rain had dispersed, and the sun was beaming from blue sky as clouds whisked out of view. In the open carriage with me were Dawn and Mr. Dabbs, whom I had chosen to ride with me for support, but also as a way to honor them for their kindness. Kort and Nemi sat behind us on a back-facing platform. Guardians on horses rode on either side, and the carriage driver was also an armed guardian. Leading the way on a magnificent steed was my love, Lurien, bedecked in military finery. Units of guardians marched in front on foot and behind, interspersed with additional carriages transporting other key figures of the queendom, including the rest of the Elemental Council, Shamus, and the advisors.

I was overwhelmed and found myself smiling, waving back, and sitting in gratitude, remembering all the people and teachers and events that came before me, all the sacrifice and pain, the courage, the determination, the open minds and hearts, including my own, that led to this surreal day. I looked up to the sky and sent a message to Ms. Bernadette that I was alive and accepting my destiny as she would have wanted, and I sent her my love and thanks. As the carriage rolled into the market plaza, I was met with a festival of abundance and harvest as it was the harvest season, the harvest moon, and the autumn equinox of balance.

As I prepared to disembark the carriage, Lurien was standing at the open door, extending a hand to help me down. Lurien was ethereal in uniform and bearing. Even their hair was styled differently that revealed both sides of their beautiful face, which was smiling at me now. I felt my foot catch in the hem of my gown in my distraction, and I started to fall from the carriage except Lurien caught me in both arms, of course, without blinking and set me with both feet on the ground. I could hear the crowd cheering. I beamed with smiles. Lurien offered an arm to escort me to the stage.

Leaning into my face, Lurien said, "I've got you, my queen." Then I felt a flicker of lips on my earlobe and heard a whisper, "You can do this, my love," before the commander pulled back and led me up the steps to the festival platform and escorted me to the throne of Demistrath.

Made in the USA
Monee, IL
21 April 2020